THE ART OF SECRETS

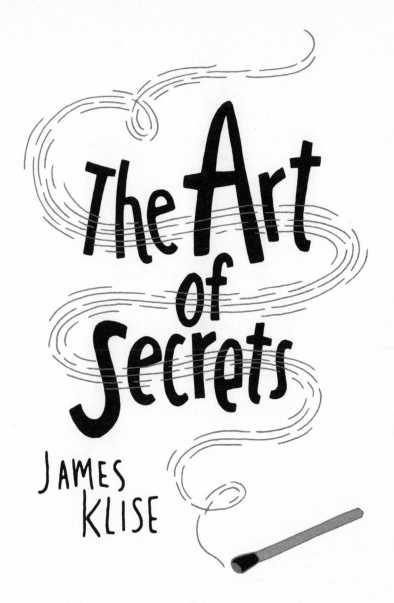

The Art of Secrets

James Klise

ALGONQUIN 2015

Published by
ALGONQUIN YOUNG READERS
an imprint of Algonquin Books of Chapel Hill
Post Office Box 2225
Chapel Hill, North Carolina 27515-2225

a division of
WORKMAN PUBLISHING
225 Varick Street
New York, New York 10014

First paperback edition, Algonquin Young Readers, April 2015. Originally
published in hardcover by Algonquin Young Readers, April 2014.
Printed in the United States of America.
Published simultaneously in Canada
by Thomas Allen & Son Limited.
Design by Connie Gabbert.

Definition of "outsider art" used with permission from Intuit: The Center
for Intuitive and Outsider Art.

Excerpt reprinted with permission of Scribner Publishing Group from *The
Great Gatsby* by F. Scott Fitzgerald. Copyright © 1925 by Charles Scribner's
Sons. Copyright renewed © 1953 by Frances Scott Fitzgerald Lanahan.

LIBRARY OF CONGRESS CATALOGING-IN-
PUBLICATION DATA
Klise, James, [date]
    The art of secrets : a novel / by James Klise
        pages cm
    Summary: When some quirky art donated to a school fundraising
effort to help a Pakistani American family, victims of a possible hate crime,
is revealed to be an unknown work by a famous outsider artist, worth
hundreds of thousands of dollars, adults and teenagers alike debate who
should get the money and begin to question each other's motivations.
    ISBN 978-1-61620-195-1 (HC)
    [1. Fund raising—Fiction. 2. Outsider art—Fiction. 3. Pakistani
Americans—Fiction. 4. Chicago (Ill.)—Fiction.] I. Title.
    PZ7.K6837Ar 2014
    [Fic]—dc23   2013043222

    ISBN 978-1-61620-482-2 (PB)

10 9 8 7 6 5 4 3 2 1
First Paperback Edition

At last, here's one just for Kate.

According to Intuit: The Center for Intuitive
and Outsider Art, in Chicago, Illinois, "outsider art" can
be defined as the "work of artists who demonstrate little
influence from the mainstream art world and who instead
are motivated by their unique personal visions."

ACT 1

Apartment fire leaves four homeless

FIRE and police crews responded to a fire that gutted a two-bedroom apartment in West Rogers Park yesterday. The three-story brick building was evacuated and no injuries were reported.

According to the Chicago Fire Department, the fire began in a first-floor unit at 6313 N. Artesian around 4:00 p.m. By 6:00 p.m., the fire was extinguished, although some smoke was still visible from the street. Smoke damage affected the units above, and the building owner reported substantial basement flooding.

Fire Department spokesperson Harry Manning said, "This was a small fire that did a lot of damage to one unit quickly." Officials are investigating the cause of the blaze.

The building is located just one block south of Devon Avenue, an area that is home to a diverse immigrant community from India and the Middle East. Onlookers gathered to watch the fire crews at work, and some reported knowing the displaced family, a couple with two children, who had occupied the rental unit for over a decade.

"It's only a tragedy," said one woman passing the scene. "Some are born under a bad star."

Another neighbor added quickly, "But this is a friendly block. We will look after this family and see they are cared for."

Chicago Tribune, **October 2**

On the evening of MONDAY, OCTOBER 29,

SABA KHAN, SOPHOMORE,

endeavors to record a few burdensome thoughts
before turning out the light.

Today at school, when the social worker asked what was "top of mind," I answered sleep. Still having a little trouble getting my stressed-out brain to shut down at night. I asked the SW if I could get a prescription — something temporary, only a few nights a week, to help to guarantee some zzz's. I know these drugs exist. I've seen the TV ads with the glow-in-the-dark bug that flies around your bedroom at night + lands on your cheek while you dream.

The SW said, "I totally get it. I have something for you." She swiveled around + rooted through a drawer in the cabinet behind her desk.

Sweet sleep at last, I thought. Yes. Bring it.

Glancing past the SW, my eyes settled on a delicate saint figurine that stands on her bookshelf. It's pretty, white glass. The lady stoops forward slightly, her eyes looking up to heaven. Or maybe she's looking up at the poster of the cartoon squirrel dangling by its tail from a tree branch. Underneath the squirrel, the words say, "Hang in there, baby! Forget about the nuts for now!"

The SW turned around + handed me . . . this notebook. She said, "You're a strong writer, yes? So if you're still having trouble sleeping, write down what's on your mind. Whatever's stressing you out. Write it all down, then put it away. You'll sleep better knowing it's all in the notebook rather than in your head."

When I asked her if she'd read it, she was like, "No, the writing is for you, a place where you can store any worries until you feel rested + ready to deal with them. The important thing is, you seem to be doing fine, all things considered."

That "all things" amused me. How impressive, I thought, that she has considered all the things.

OK . . . so I asked the SW for a magical, ethereal, glow-in-the-dark bug + she gave me this ordinary spiral-bound notebook. She hadn't said the word "journal," which was genius, because I refuse to journal. I'm no Anne Frank. Anne Frank did not have a laptop or the Internet—but then, ugh, neither do I anymore. This notebook is not what I wanted, but it is 10 o'clock already + there's a long night ahead + I'm desperate.

So here goes.

First of all, people at school need to review some simple facts. Everybody saw us in the park, at the tennis courts. The coaches saw us. My teammates saw us. Witnesses have provided statements on our behalf. Can a person be in 2 places at once?

Let the record show: My whole family was at the park on the afternoon of October 1, watching me completely destroy my opponent from Fenwick, a bony white girl with a weak grip + no sense of play. It definitely helped that I was rocking the new shorter haircut, the ends curling just past my shoulders, so that when I wore the yellow/red sweatband across my forehead, the girls laughed + said, "Look out—yo, it's Wonder Woman!" I loved it. I grabbed my racket + owned that court. As everyone knows, Day 1 after a new haircut is the most powerful day.

Just like everyone knows that while I, Wonder Woman, kicked that Fenwick girl's butt on the center court, way across town a fire destroyed everything in our apartment. I saw the pictures afterward. Our kitchen furniture looked scary—black + lumpy, like chicken wings that have been left on a grill for too long.

We lost everything, 15 years of stuff. Photographs sent from Pakistan + the jewelry Ammi brought in a cardboard suitcase when she + Papa first came to this country.

15 years of my family's history, destroyed in under 2 hours.

4 weeks later, people are still looking at us funny. Nobody comes straight out + asks the blaming questions: How could

5

you let that happen? How irresponsible can you people be? Or—who did you piss off? Nobody asks, but the accusations are plain on their faces. Sometimes I think people want to hold victims responsible for the bad things that happen to them.

Cartoon squirrel is right. Forget about the nuts for now!

[She puts the notebook on the floor next to the bed and turns out the light.]

[Forty minutes later, she turns the light on again and opens the notebook.]

Also: The newspaper described all of us—the whole neighborhood—as "immigrants." We are Americans! I was born at Swedish Covenant Hospital on Foster Avenue. So was Salman. He's only 6 + already he wants to be a U.S. Marine. Ammi + Papa did the paperwork, passed the citizen tests + took the oath. They probably know more about the U.S. Constitution than most parents at school. Papa splits Bulls season tickets with some guys at the factory, so he gets to see 5 Bulls games every winter. He's obsessed! Meanwhile, Ammi loves other American games: Clue, Yahtzee, Pictionary, Pit. It was like a sickness with the mothers in our old building, this bizarre fever for playing box games meant for kids.

I admit, I do feel <u>more</u> American than them, if that even makes sense. Maybe because Salman + I are citizens by birth,

6

we're less traditional. They still dress like they did before they came here. I never wear the salwar kameez unless it's a holiday or we have visitors from Pakistan. On school days, it's fine with Ammi that I leave my dupattas at home in a drawer — in general, headscarves are not my personal choice — but I like having the option. When I take off my worthless school uniform, I dress the same as my friends — jeans, T-shirts, stretchy tops, even sweatshirts when it gets cold.

But I'm a good person. I work hard. I pray when I'm supposed to. I fast when the calendar says to. I try to be thoughtful, generous + respectful. My guess is, Ammi + Papa are as proud of me as they are of Salman.

Sometimes, like any of my friends, I have to negotiate. Last year, when I decided to join the tennis team, Papa pitched a fit. He didn't like the idea of me going out in shorts, exposing my legs to the eyes of strangers. "You are 14," he told me at the time, "not a little girl anymore." Ammi convinced him to let me play. "It is good to be strong," she reasoned at supper. Later she whispered to me, "Plus, when you win at something, it puts color in your cheek."

Papa finally agreed, but only under the condition that I wear sweatpants when I play. He never liked the team T-shirts. "Too revealing," he said. He always says that. Too revealing.

"Why is the T-shirt too revealing?" I asked him. "What do we have to protect? My sacred elbows?"

He smiled. "No," he said. "Not your lovely elbows."

7

"Scaly ugly elbows!" teased Salman from the sofa.

I was super annoyed at both of them. "What then? What is there to protect?"

Papa took off his wire-rimmed glasses, as he does whenever he wants us to stare into his big dark eyes + really listen to him. There are times when Papa looks at me + he seems to see more than just me. "Your innocence," he answered finally, "as well as the innocence of others."

I fully acknowledge that Ammi + Papa have taken huge risks + sacrificed everything for us. + sure, when I play tennis, I wear a loose T-shirt to please them. But I'm not the same as them. Sometimes I don't want to negotiate. The fact is, I'm not the innocent kid they think I am.

If only they knew.

In a way, the fire might have been the best thing that ever happened to me. But maybe even writing that is t.o.o. r.e.v.e.a.l.i.n.g.

FAROOQ KHAN, U.S. CITIZEN,

"America, land of opportunities." That's what we always heard in Pakistan, yes? All the opportunities to be found in America. Khawla and I laugh about it now, somewhat bitterly.

Opportunities, for example, like years of hard work in a factory, where I put shampoo bottles into shipping boxes.

Opportunities like the flames of a merciless fire that take away all the things we save my wages for.

Opportunities like *tennis*?

I did not play tennis in Pakistan. The first time I held a tennis ball in my hand, it was one my daughter, Saba, brought home. I did not expect its texture to be furry and soft, like an odd, neon-green fruit.

I went to all of Saba's tennis matches. If my daughter was going into the world wearing nothing but a T-shirt, I wanted the world to know I was there to protect her.

My wife went also, because she loves to watch Saba play. Saba is graceful, strong, and smart on the court. I admit there is something soothing about watching the ball sailing back and forth over the net; nothing but the sound of the ball hitting the racket, then the court, and the squeak and scuffle of rubber-soled shoes. When two opponents are playing well, it is almost like a prayer to watch. Excellence in all forms honors God.

Khawla and I went to every match, never missing one. We sat on the hood of our Ford sedan and watched from the parking lot, while our son, Salman, read library books in the front seat, or played with the dashboard—played at driving, a normal childhood fantasy, yes?

As the tennis season progressed, summer ended and fall arrived. The trees that surrounded the courts turned yellow, orange, and red—fiery, you could say. In retrospect, like an omen.

At the last match, against Fenwick, my wife found a vending machine and purchased a small bag of barbecue-flavored potato chips. We shared them during the match. "Delicious," we agreed.

"Not as good as Pringles," Khawla decided.

We eat the junk food. Sometimes we watch American television. Every Fourth of July, we picnic with the rest of Chicago at the lakeshore, waiting for the pinwheels and starbursts to appear over the water after dark.

Until the fire, we made our home in a two-bedroom apartment in a handsome brick building with a courtyard. A crowded, safe area, not trendy or expensive. Streets filled with people like us who came to this country in search of the best opportunities for our children.

Opportunities—how we clung to that word! It is a dreamer's word.

After Saba's tennis match, we drove back to that apartment, with no idea of the inferno that awaited us. Khawla and I discussed supper, listing the ordinary, usual things that would be waiting for us in the cupboard. "If only we had more of the barbecue chips," I said.

"Children, listen," my wife laughed, "your father is a cowboy now."

We approached our street, and my daughter remarked that the air smelled funny, like smoke from a fire.

A police SUV blocked the entrance to our street, lights flashing. And then we could see, farther down the block, the long red trucks.

My son became excited, overly so, as he does whenever he sees a fire truck. "Fire, fire!"

We parked and got out of the car. Our eyes followed the direction of the fire hoses, first to our own building, then incredulously to where our own windows would be—but here oddly open, black-rimmed, bold dancing flames inside. No longer like windows, but like three smoky wood ovens in a row.

The blaze was contained to our unit, everything charred in a flash. The rest of the building was spared, except for the smoke and water damage.

We had nothing left. Nothing but our rusty old Ford. Even Salman's books were from the library.

The fire marshal told us the fire might have been started

on purpose. "It burned so fast," he said. He used the word *arson*. He promised an investigation.

Arson.

My wife spoke up, saying this was impossible. We have no enemies in this country, nor in the one we left behind. We have only friends.

Her words were proven true by the swift offers of places to stay, friends from this mosque, neighbors. The community gathered around us, lifted us. Overnight a calendar was created, a weekly schedule of beds and meals, opportunities to donate food and furniture, all for us. I can hardly believe it myself, but starting tonight my family will sleep in a high-rise, luxury condominium with a view of Lake Michigan. Temporary, of course, but *free,* donated by a family at my daughter's school. The angels have cared for us.

And yet despite these blessings, or perhaps because of them, I have lived in a kind of misery these past weeks. I am a man who may have lost much more than the physical objects in his home.

[He removes his eyeglasses, placing them on the table between him and the imam.]

I have been carrying a secret—a burden I want to share with you now, so that this black spot on my conscience may be removed and I can pray again with a clean heart.

When the fire marshal told us that the fire might have been started on purpose, a sickening dread washed over my body, a suspicion that with all my strength I struggled to

12

conceal. My eyes met the eyes of my son, and I realized with a paralyzing fear the likelihood that the arsonist was not an enemy to my family but my own innocent boy who has fallen prey to the seductive power of fire.

There were two occasions at tennis matches, our backs momentarily turned from him, when Salman had toyed with the cigarette lighter in the car, poking bits of paper and sticks at it to see how quickly smoke would appear. We could smell the smoke from where we sat. His mother slapped his fingers and took to keeping him on the grass where she could watch him.

Then late one night, only a week before the apartment fire, I found my son sitting in our kitchen, using a wooden match from the stove to set fire to a plastic toy soldier. He claimed to be repairing the figure, refastening its head by melting the plastic. I scolded him, but did not punish him for it. The Prophet said that a strong man controls his anger. But now I worry . . . this series of small events, this danger-ous fascination . . .

In front of the fire marshal, I could not voice these fears. I cannot even discuss this suspicion with my wife. The fire has distressed the woman enough.

Today a member of the fire department visited me at the factory, accompanied by a police officer. They were friendly to me, but the news was not good. The initial investigation has confirmed that the fire was started with rags soaked in turpentine. Arson.

I listened and said nothing. What could I have said?

STEVE DAVINSKI, SENIOR,

*leads a tour of the Highsmith School, a reputable yet no-
longer-selective private high school, where Saba Khan
also is a student.*

Good morning, folks. Thanks for coming out on a day like this.

While we wait, everybody please take care to avoid the H there on the floor. This is our school seal. The H stands for Highsmith, of course, and also for Honor. This is considered a sacred spot on campus, a common belief shared by all students, so we need to watch our—

Ma'am? If you could . . . move your bag a tiny bit, please? Thanks.

I agree, the campus is very cool, especially since we are so close to the Loop. Some of the buildings are over a hundred years old. Visitors may like how everything looks, but students mostly complain about climbing stairs. Half the campus is stairs!

Can everybody hear me? Yeah, I know you all can *see* me. That's probably why they gave me this job.

[He smirks, in response to small, polite laughter
from the crowd.]

I am "physically conspicuous," one might say. Or "ver-
tically enhanced." Kids around here call me Da-*vine*-ski,
since I'm like a vine, you know? Always growing.

Obviously I'm not wearing my uniform today, since it's
Saturday. During the week, all Highsmith students wear a
standard uniform: dress shirts and khaki pants, belt required,
no tennis shoes. Men wear the signature Highsmith necktie,
which, depending on who you ask, is either the color of our
sacred honor or the color of all the dark red things that could
possibly stain a young man's tie in the cafeteria.

Nobody likes wearing the uniform, of course, but even
I admit it's for the best. Highsmith welcomes a few lucky
students on need-based scholarships every year, always has.
The idea behind the uniform is that we all dress the same,
no matter what kind of job our parents have, and by grad-
uation, we've all had the same valuable opportunities. By
then, most of us have a stain or two on our neckties. I mean,
we're only human!

Please try to stick close as we move around campus, so I
don't have to yell so much. Sometimes after tours, my voice
sounds like it's been through a blender. That's not good for
someone like me. Trust me, I like to talk.

[He takes out a piece of paper and reads.]

15

"In 1911, The Highsmith School was created by Chicago's wealthiest citizens with an initial endowment of five hundred thousand dollars."

[Looks up from the paper.]

I'm a numbers guy, folks, and no kidding, that was a pile of money back then. I guess it still is, to most of us.

[Goes back to reading.]

"Originally the school consisted of only the building we are standing in, but we have grown over the decades and now the campus has a total of four buildings, including the gymnasium, which remains the largest stand-alone school gymnasium in the city of Chicago."

[Looks up from the paper.]

Seriously, wait until you see it. If you're thinking of coming here, you should definitely come to one of our basketball games this winter. Actually, I'm starting center on the varsity team, so, I mean . . . that's pretty cool, right?

*[Waits for some perfunctory applause
before going back to reading.]*

"Highsmith's founders believed that a fine school required a handsome campus, no matter how expensive to maintain.

They were convinced that the best education—the most progressive thinking—occurs in a beautiful setting. Think back to ancient Greece and Rome, the splendor of Egypt, or the great renovation of Paris during the reign of Napoleon III. All the most advanced thinking took place during a time of revolutionary architectural design—"

Excuse me? Ma'am, could you speak up, please?

[Takes a deep breath.]

Wow . . . wow. You heard about that? Holy cats, that is some fast-moving information. If only my guys were that speedy on the court.

Well, okay, yes, there has been some whispering the past couple of days about what we might call . . . a discovery . . . here at Highsmith. Something exciting is going on, and I understand your curiosity.

However, it is totally premature for us to discuss that topic today. There's no confirmation yet, so at this time— I mean, *at any time*, it would be wrong for us to speculate about other people's business. We all agree on that, I'm sure.

Sorry if this disappoints you, ma'am, but we will not be seeing any *strange watercolor paintings* on this tour today. This is a school, after all, not an art museum, and that's where the administration wants to keep the focus for now.

Okay, then . . . Exit's right over there. Have a good day, ma'am.

Folks, please don't think I'm being rude or anything, but

we're here this morning to talk about the school. Clubs, traditions, that kind of stuff.

So, yeah.

Did I mention I'm senior class president? Three years in a row. "Three-peat!" everybody said, last time I got elected.

DA-VINE-SKI CLINGS TO OFFICE, the headline said.

Yeah, that was pretty cool.

Now if we can continue. . . . By the way, we'll be seeing only two of the buildings on the tour. The other two don't get used so much anymore. Enrollment's been down, to be honest, so we're glad you're here!

Please follow me. Careful again, folks, not to step on the H. . . .

JAVIER CONEJERA, SOPHOMORE,

uses a library computer to write to his friend Jennifer in
Oklahoma. Inadvertently, he uses the workstation that
is reserved for catalog searches only.

A mi hermana Americana—

Now I am in Chicago, and I remember our good
times last year. Now maybe I understand what you
felt when you lived with my family in España. Now I
am the toad from a different well!

You will laugh because I walk the streets here
holding the GPS that my host family gives to me. I
make all the turns the GPS announces. Somewhat
embarrassing, yes, but in this way I see all the
corners of this brutal, incredible city.

I tell you some things on the phone, but for others
it is better to send via email, because I do not want
my host family to learn them. Jen, this family is very
strange. They are busy with the activities to the

19

extreme, too busy to know me. I am alone in the house too often—and ay, the house! I do not have words to describe. In this place, the closets and cupboards cannot store the useful objects because they are so filled with the discarded objects. The most important object is the big calendar that tells the family where they need to be at all times. The calendar is in the kitchen. (Not in the "chicken"—I confuse these words at least one time every day!)

Do you remember, last year P. Hector told our class: "Admire the peacock, so beautiful in the garden. But if you invite it into the house, it will shit on the rug." The truth is, my host family brings many peacocks into the house.

However . . . Maybe there is value to the numerous things people keep. For example, at the school, a student named Saba Khan lost her apartment in a terrible fire. We all saw this tragedy on the television. The people included the story on Facebook. This family lost it all, aside from their lives. The father works in a factory. Two children. Very sad.

Then in the recent days I see posters around the school, asking for all the people to bring things to sell. An auction to benefit this family of Khans.

The date for the event is the 15 of December. The "season of giving," no? Many families have donated items for the auction. Extra items from the home, or special items. My host family donated a membership to a golf society. Mr. Hamilton, the teacher of music, donated tickets to the symphony of Chicago. Mrs. Langford, the teacher of psychology, donated five bottles of wine in a basket. All the money raised will go to this family.

Last week my classmate Kendra asked if I will donate items to the auction. I told her, "Very sorry, but I have nothing to give." I felt ashamed, because I have admired this blonde, bold girl very much. One day I asked her for help, and she proofread my essay with such care, as if the work is hers. She helped me earn a B on the essay. Now she asked for help in return. She poked me with her notebook and smiled. "Javier," she told me, gentle but firm, "all the people have something to give."

When she told me this, I felt two things at the same time. First, a burden—a responsibility that I did not believe was mine. But also, like sudden rain falling over the head, this sense of belonging. Kendra suggested that I am part of the community, too, only because I am here in Chicago, present. And that feels like a dream coming true.

However, how can I help? I told her, "I came to this country with two suitcases."

"I have the answer!" she told me very loud. "Spanish. Six free lessons or tutoring sessions, taught by a native speaker. That will be your donation." She wrote it down before I found words to respond.

To disappoint such a girl—Jen, this is impossible. She represents beauty on the inside and on the outside. She is tall, and the long hair is straight and light, like the Danish girls who come to our beach. The eyes are pale and sparkle like the sea waves. She is smiling whenever I see her, and that makes me smile, too. Maybe Kendra will be a friend for me in this city.

I feel lonely still, but also grateful to have the opportunity to spend this school year observing these people. My dream always was to come and study in the U.S. I see how the Americans are on TV—so many groups of friends. Here I want to collect the friends the way my great-grandmother collects the brown sweaters, remember? You know how difficult it is for me always in situations that are social.

Well, it requires so much time to write to you in this manner. I wish we could Skype. That way we can see each other and talk about ordinary, boring matters, as we once did. I am eager to see you at the spring holiday!

I must go now. Several students wait to use this computer, even though others are free to be used. :\

Also, to help pay for my ticket to see you, I have taken a job in the school cafeteria (in the "kitchen," "kitchen," "kitchen," not in the "chicken"). The job is good because it puts me with people, and not always in the house of my host family.

With love from your Spanish brother—now in Chicago! ☺

Later that morning,

DR. REGINA STICKMAN, PRINCIPAL,

welcomes a reporter from the Chicago Tribune
into her spacious, wood-paneled office.

Fantastic, I am thrilled you're here.

Is your umbrella dripping? Put it—wait, sorry, not on the rug. We got that carpet last year, and I spend half my day protecting it from muddy shoes.

Thank you. Please sit down.

I hope the traffic wasn't awful. The one-way streets in this neighborhood can be a bit of a puzzle. They take some getting used to.

Anyhow, I won't waste your time. Like I told you on the phone, you've got one hell of a story here. This is one of those feel-good stories that don't happen often enough, but people love to read about.

What's happening this month says something important about the school culture here. You should stress that when you write the article. It's no accident this incredible story is unfolding right here at Highsmith. All the time, I tell prospective parents that our curriculum is designed to make ordinary students into extraordinary citizens. Based on what's happening now, we are succeeding! Let me tell you, that truly warms the heart of this seen-it-all-before school administrator. I mean, you have no idea.

In my view, your story—or maybe it's a series of stories—will highlight the remarkable things that are happening. If we can get something on the editorial page, so much the better, because those are the readers with money to spend, am I right?

One of the things you want to stress is that the fundraising has been student driven. *Teens* are leading this effort—young people who make us all hopeful for the future. I'll make sure you get access to them. Here, I'm writing down names for you. Also, you'll want to talk to Jean Delacroix in the Art Department, who was the one who noticed last week that nothing short of a *miracle* may have fallen into our laps.

Naturally I cannot share any particulars about Saba Khan or her time here at Highsmith. The law protects her privacy. You seem like a nice person, and I'm eager to work with you on this project. But I simply cannot discuss any personal details about Saba or her family.

Besides, your paper has already covered that aspect of the story. A little too much, if you'll excuse my opinion. There are children involved. This fire was no accident, I get that. And off the record, I can see that it makes the family look bad. Arson? Whatever the motive, no one wants to be associated with a story like that—including me, to be perfectly honest.

25

Also, like I'm telling you, an apartment fire is not the story. The real story here is the inspiring *response* to the fire. You want readers to learn about the incredible things taking place in the aftermath of this sad event.

[Standing and moving toward the door.]

All right, then? I'm giving you full access. Feel free to wander around and ask any questions you want about the fundraiser next month. That said, I do ask that you avoid putting anyone in an awkward position. Let's leave Saba out of this. Young people are helpful by nature, and having to say "no" is unpleasant for anybody. I'm sure you understand.

Too bad it's so ugly outside. Will you be sending a photographer? Obviously I'd love for you to get some shots of the campus. In a pinch, I might have something you can use—the lagoon in springtime, maybe, surrounded by the orange day lilies, or . . . no? You're right—you'll get what you need. *No hurry.* The auction's more than a month away. Besides, the campus looks spectacular when it's covered in snow, and we can cross our fingers for that.

Thanks again for your visit. No, thank *you!*

KENDRA SPOON, SOPHOMORE,

*at her locker. On one arm, Kendra balances a tray
of sugar cookies decorated with pink icing.*

Yeah, that's me. If you can hold on a sec . . . ?

Okay, I'm not sure what to say. I'm more comfortable in a behind-the-scenes, stuffing-envelopes kind of role. I'm not a spokesperson or anything. Maybe you can talk to my brother, Kevin? He's a senior. Seniors should be in the cafeteria by now. Go that way and turn left at the school seal. You'll know it when you see it—the big red H on the floor. To me, it looks a little bit like a body outline at a crime scene.

If I can just say . . . I *like* Saba. No one's got a problem with Saba. I was on the tennis team with her. And so to me . . . I mean, can you imagine losing everything you have? This family needs help. Someone needs to help them. If we can make sure they're better off *after* the fire than before—that's the only way any of this will make sense. We can make this story turn out okay.

Sir, I don't mean to be rude, but I gotta run to Spanish. We're having a *fiesta de cumpleaños* for this girl, Kristin. In class, we call her Marta, because that makes perfect sense.

Do you want a cookie?

*Minutes later, in a crowded cafeteria
that reeks of grease and disinfectant,*

KEVIN SPOON, SENIOR,

*pulls two chairs together so that he may speak
at length with the reporter.*

No problem, well, thanks for helping us to promote the fundraiser. The auction date will be December fifteenth, right
here at school. That's a Saturday. It starts at ten in the morning. Obviously, you want to talk to the art teacher—

Why did I get involved?

Oh man . . . The thing is, my family relocated here in
June. We're new to Chicago, but not new to the *situation* of
being new. My mom sells air. It's our family joke. Whenever she's long-winded or going on about some crazy thing,
my sister or I will whisper: "*Psst*—Mom sells air."

But she really does! She sells commercial ad spots on the
radio. You want thirty seconds of air during the morning
rush hour? It will cost you.

My mom is awesome at sales. No joke, Monica Spoon
could sell milk to cows. People like her. We've lived all over
the country, mostly towns, but Chicago's the big league.
The bigger the market, the higher her commission.

Moving to a new place is never easy, but Kendra and I are

pros at it by now. When you're new, you join all the teams, and you bake the cookies, and you hustle like crazy. And maybe in this case, you help to organize a benefit for a family of complete strangers. You *want* people to *like* you, you know? That's something my mom always drilled into us.

Besides, my sister has some classes with Saba Khan. They're both on the tennis team. To Kendra, Saba isn't just a name attached to a random tragedy in the newspaper.

I wish I could say the auction was our idea, but it was my mom's. My mom is . . . Put it this way, she's a big dreamer. Freaking huge imagination. Just between you and me, she's got a couple of screenplay drafts in a drawer somewhere, in case the whole "sales thing" doesn't work out for her.

So at breakfast the day after the fire, Kendra was reading one of the newspaper stories about the Khans. She just about spilled her OJ with excitement, and said something like, "Look, even her initials are the same as mine. Saba Khan, Kendra Spoon, just reversed. Doesn't that seem like a sign?"

I said it sounded like a flaky sign to me.

"Good enough," my mom said. "Flaky signs often guide us in the right direction."

And seriously, within minutes, the whole thing appeared in my mom's head like a movie trailer, and she was literally *performing* for us while we ate our oatmeal. She was like, "Picture an auction scene, okay, which is always fabulous in a movie. Very suspenseful, right? And everybody is gathered in the school gym, a gigantic crowd, parents, students, teachers—"

I mumbled to Kendra, "Maybe a few rich people, too."

Mom frowned at me, I guess for interrupting her flow. "Obviously rich people, Kevin, that's the whole flipping point. Right? But the Khans would be sitting in the front row. The spotlight is on them, naturally, because *this is the day that will change their lives forever.*"

Kendra said maybe we could take a dry-erase board from a classroom and set it up near the auctioneer so that someone could write down the sale prices with a gigantic red marker, adding them up in a column that would keep getting longer and longer.

And Mom was like, "Yes, Kendra! Good! Can't you imagine the faces on Saba and her family? Imagine the close-up where you can *totally see* in the eyes of these people how much this money is going to mean for them . . ."

This was so typical of my mom. I mean, like I said, the woman sells air. I assumed this grand inspiration would blow over like all the others. But when we got home from school that night, Mom was still talking her way through the script. The funniest part was that, by then, in her mind, *Kendra and I* were the leads, not the Khans! We would lead the whole thing. Please tell me that's completely normal "mom" behavior.

Just to be clear: My sister may *look* like my mom, but that's where the similarities end. Kendra's not flaky at all. More than anybody I know, Kendra believes in her personal power to improve the world. She's always been that way. I give her credit for taking Mom's lunatic ranting and making it practical and real. And for making *me* believe that we could really do something to help.

Also, for Kendra . . . I mean, there are other motives. It looks like our family will be in Chicago for a while, so Kendra may actually get three years at Highsmith. As sad as it sounds, and my sister will never admit this, Saba's tragedy is Kendra's social opportunity. It's barely November and people know who my sister is . . . and they *like* her, you know? All because of this auction project.

Wait—please don't put that last part in the paper. That sounds cold. Best way to put it is, Kendra and I want to help this family. The whole school does. It's no big mystery, it's not crop circles. It just feels good to help people, right? It's the decent thing to do. That's where we're coming from.

The following day, in the faculty lunchroom,
the ham salad of

WENDY PINCH,
DEPARTMENT OF PHYSICAL EDUCATION,

sits untouched so that she might get something
off her chest, which is sizeable.

Excuse me—if I may say something?

Thirty years, that's how long I've been teaching here.
More than your age, some of you. The little turds we deal
with now? Twenty-five years ago, I taught their little-turd
parents. When I was a student at Highsmith, I sat in desks
next to their little-turd grandparents.

In lots of cases, the problem you observe with a student
is the same problem I have observed with generations of
that family. Behavior problems, laziness, cheating, sexual
acting-out—these can be *family traits*, see? And no matter
what color their skin, or what religion they claim to pro-
fess, rich kids, poor kids, smart kids and the dumb ones,
god bless 'em, one thing they have in common is that they're
all exactly like their parents. It's the apples-and-trees thing,
you got me?

Hell, we see it on report-card nights. That moment

when we meet a loco parent and think, *Ah-HA, well THIS explains everything!*

And knowing this, see, makes it hard to sit here and listen to you guys still speculating about what may have happened at the Khans' apartment. Who cares *how* it happened? A family lost a home. Can't we leave it at that?

All that matters to me is, Saba Khan's a good kid. Honestly that's why I bawled so hard after the fire. It wasn't like this awful thing happened to some stuck-up little princess. No, it happened to one of the truly *nice* ones. Doesn't seem fair, see? Every time I'm with poor Saba, it's all I can do to stop from hugging the stuffing out of her.

Maybe her situation gets to me because we've spent time together. Two years on my tennis team. Not chatty, but respectful. She works at her game. The kid doesn't even have a racket of her own. Takes one from the bucket in the gym office. Always the same one. Nothing special about the thing, but everyone knows the pink Wilson hybrid goes to Saba.

Plus, her parents never miss a match. Gotta love that support. You see it with these first-generation families.

The Spoon kids are impressive, too. I only met the mother once, at one of the summer registration nights. She sort of marched into the gym—you know the type—straight from work, lipstick and pearls, serious shoes. Pretty conservative, I was guessing, or at least works in that environment. She picked up her kids' schedules like she was doing me a favor. All business, no small talk. Still, she had a spark about her, a *spark*, like she can get things done.

So I'm not surprised that her kids are pretty terrific. They've got that spark, too. They stand out without even trying—blond hair, what they call "all American" looks. Kevin, the senior, to give him credit, the kid's an excellent athlete. He knows how to move the ball down the court. And he's *smart*, see? Some kids, you've got to remind them, every practice, what their strengths and weaknesses are. Steve Davinski, for example. He's a giant, one of my starters. He can practically dunk the ball without lifting his arms. But he can only see what's in front of him; he can only see the *now*.

Kevin Spoon, on the other hand—he understands cause and effect. I can count on him to see an opportunity on the court *before the opportunity exists*. Remarkable kid. Face it, not many boys can transfer in senior year and make the varsity team. Coaches spend a couple of seasons building this well-oiled machine. You add a new element like Kevin Spoon and it's a risk. Wild card. But Kevin showed up for conditioning last month, ready to show me what he could do. I found out later he was varsity at the last two schools he attended, too. Four different schools, three varsity teams. See, that's impressive.

That's not just talent, it's determination. Maybe all that moving around has taught him to look way far ahead. He knows that winning one game doesn't really matter. What matters is the game he'll be playing next year. If a kid like Kevin has vision, it can carry him to where he wants to be.

The sister, Kendra, she's on my tennis team. Very polite, friendly, but fierce on the court. Not hot dogs, these

Spoons, not needy. They don't need that kind of attention. They just want to get the job done.

These are nice kids, all three of them. That means *good parents*.

Talk all you want, but you won't hear me say a word against 'em.

On *WEDNESDAY, NOVEMBER 7,*
on the back of a Human Resources flier that outlines
smart precautions to take during cold-and-flu season,

FAROOQ KHAN, U.S. CITIZEN,

writes a list of prayer intentions for the coming days.

1. OFFER PRAYERS OF GRATITUDE THAT WE HAVE REMAINED SAFE
    DURING THIS CRISIS.

2. RECOGNIZE BEFORE GOD THAT I AM RESPONSIBLE FOR MY
    FAMILY—FOR ALL MEMBERS OF MY FAMILY, AND FOR THEIR
    ACTIONS.

3. ASK FOR THE HELP OF GOD AND HIS ANGELS TO PROVE
    SALMAN INNOCENT OF SETTING THE FIRE, SO THAT OUR
    HEARTS MAY BE CLEAN.

4. EVEN IF SALMAN IS RESPONSIBLE FOR THIS FOOLISH AND SERIOUS
    CRIME, PRAY THAT MY WIFE AND DAUGHTER REMAIN INNOCENT
    IN THE EYES OF GOD, AND SO MAY THEIR ANGELS TESTIFY.

5. MOREOVER, IF SALMAN IS TRULY GUILTY OF THIS CRIME,
    PRAY THAT GOD WILL HEAR MY ACCOUNT ON THE DAY OF
    JUDGMENT AND WILL FORGIVE A MAN WHO SUSPECTED THE
    TRUTH, BUT CHOSE TO REMAIN SILENT.

6. PRAY THAT MY FAMILY WILL NOT BE PUNISHED FOR RECEIVING THE GOOD THINGS PROVIDED BY MY COMMUNITY AT THIS TIME OF CRISIS, EVEN WHEN WE MAY BE RESPONSIBLE FOR THE CRISIS OURSELVES.

7. PROMISE TO PLEDGE EVEN MORE ZAKAT FOR THE POOR, ACCORDING TO HOW MUCH $$ THE AUCTION RAISES FOR US.

8. PRAY THAT MY FAMILY IS KEPT SAFE FROM ALL WINTER SICKNESS.

That evening, after completing the
work in a chemistry book chapter called
"Forces, Electrons and Bonds,"

SABA KHAN, SOPHOMORE,

directs her attention to matters less theoretical,
more practical.

My angel Beti got a new phone + gave me her old one! She says I need it because I'm "notorious," not only because of the fire. I told her to get out of town—but if you can't believe your BFFL, who can you believe?

Imagine that before all this craziness began, my bold girl Beti had stood in the Highsmith caf + addressed the student body. (Which, in fact, she would gladly do. Beti thinks public speaking is in her blood, because 100 years ago her grandparents had a radio show in the Philippines.) Anyway, if Beti had asked, "Classmates, do you know Saba Khan?" the 3 most popular answers would have been, "Sorry," "No idea," + "Never heard of her." Or maybe, "Is she one of those scarf girls?"

Uh, negative. I take a very immodest pride in my hair.

Sometimes I wear it down, sometimes I pin it back. Every morning before school, I smile into my bedroom mirror + ask: What shall I do with these gorgeous shiny tresses today?

What a colossal waste of time. Did I really think my shorter haircut would help? All that research, all those magazines. Nobody noticed.

I do accept blame for my former invisibility. I stayed quiet, smiled constantly like the village idiot + avoided conflict. My goal? To survive my lovely Highsmith experience without any emotional scarring. I was happy to coast. The idea of being popular was so far from reality that I honestly never considered it a possibility. My girls + I hang out at school, eat lunch together, share notes, etc—but when it comes to parties + weekend stuff, I'm stuck at home, always within view of Ammi's watchdog eyes.

"Wait, is she one of the scarf girls?"

I've had my Facebook account forever. 2 months ago, I had 34 friends. A few from homeroom, girls on the tennis team—a flurry of friendly camaraderie when I first opened the account.

Then this chemistry experiment: We added fire.

Today on Beti's old/my new phone, I checked Facebook: 752 friend requests. At this rate, I'll have more than 1000 FBFs by the end of the month, mostly kids I've never met. Thanks to updates, I now know more about some of these random people than I do about my own squirrelly brother.

The opposite of invisible is not simply visible. The opposite of invisible is _prominent_. Without even meaning to, that's what I've become. The fire put me dead center on the school social map.

Before the fire, I took pride in 3 things: 1) my tennis game, which is fierce + always getting better, 2) my hair, which is naturally wavy _yet still_ does what I tell it to, and 3) my freakishly small hands, which Ammi tells me are a good thing, a family trait—"delicate but strong" + they do look spectacular when she hennas them for my birthday every summer.

Since the fire, I have a new kind of pride. In any school, kids cluster around the girl who's at the center of all the drama. Now they mob me at the bus stop. They invite me to parties. Complete strangers stop at my locker to "check in," ask how I'm doing.

It's a weird kind of popular, I guess. Popularity by pity. But no weirder than other ways of getting noticed—being pretty, having money, hooking up. Most of us will take it any way we can. My girls Beti + Danielle are down with it, for sure. "Ride it out," they say, "see where it takes you."

Come one, come all. Please join me in the spotlight! Everybody's invited. _Friend me!_

And then there's Mr. STEVE. Possibly the strangest +

definitely the most radical way the fire changed my life: "In a relationship with Steve Davinski." Now that would be a status update!

Only I would never, ever put that on Facebook. I couldn't risk having Ammi + Papa find out.

Also, is that status precisely, technically accurate?

Even before I met Steve, I knew who he was. He's bigger than life. He moves around the school like a grinning, curly-haired giant, surrounded by his less attractive minions — the constant traveling wall of Steve Davinski.

For a long time, I didn't give him much thought. He was just the infamous "Steve 'the creeping vine' Da-vine-ski."

+ so when he first said hello . . . I figured he might be one of those people who are attracted to drama, too. After all, he's 6'9". He is, like, genetically designed to be the center of attention.

+ one day, at that classic romantic campus spot known as "Tarzan's Shack," Steve glanced in my direction. + for whatever reason at all, he decided to shine that goofy charm all over me.

I actually felt skeptical when he approached me. He's a senior. He could have any straight girl in the school. Plus, I heard what the girls said: He's like a weed, he takes over, he "chokes all the life around him," . . . all that.

But hey, I like cute boys. I'm not exactly immune to how fine his butt looks in those dorky khakis.

41

The fire took everything from my family. But the funny thing is, it also gave me things, like Beti's phone. It gave me a new identity at school. It gave me Steve.

The girls say it's time I stop questioning it. Ride it out, see where it takes me . . . + maybe even . . . enjoy it!

Meanwhile, in a basement rec room
strewn with Nerf balls, pool cues and an impressive
array of video game equipment,

STEVE DAVINSKI, SENIOR,

shares some brotherly wisdom
with Don Davinski, age 11.

For me, bro, the easiest thing in the world is getting a girl to like me. Simple as when ole "Da-*vine*-ski" drops basketballs through the net. Simple as winning student government elections.

Not everyone can do these things, I guess. But to me they feel as natural as slipping feet into size 16 shoes. I'm guessing it will be that way for you, too, someday.

I'm not bragging, Dawg. You should watch me, learn from me. Seduction of the opposite sex is simple. It's a combination of three things: logic, practice, and strategy. It really works, you can be confident. And *confidence* is one of the major factors that make a person look *super hot* in the eyes of other people.

Logic, practice, strategy—write those down, why don't you?

So get this: About a month ago, I found this chick Saba Khan sitting alone outside, in a part of campus called

43

Tarlan's Track. We all call it "Tarzan's Shack," but you get fined a quarter if any teacher hears you. The Shack is pretty cool. Some hippie doctor named Tarlan built it for gym classes about a billion years ago. Basically it's these jungle gyms and high-ropes equipment constructed in a big old circle. Nowadays it's totally neglected and covered in ivy, but it's still pretty cool. I'll show it to you sometime.

Anyway, I'd heard Saba sometimes hung out there during free periods, and I went looking for her. In the fall, the ivy on the rusted bars turns bright red. And this babe was sitting there, alone, surrounded by this color, doing her math homework.

Actually she's one of those girls you might not notice if you aren't looking for her, but once you see her, you realize she's pretty. Pretty-like-a-picture, I mean, rather than pretty-like-a-hot-girl-in-a-music-video. She's on the quiet side, but it's like . . . maybe she knows she doesn't need to make a lot of noise to get your attention. She always has this little grin that suggests she's keeping a secret. Plus, she's got the kind of hair Mom would say is "lovely" just because it's shiny and thick, but the way she lets it curve around her face just adds to the mystery.

For a week, the whole school had been talking about Saba, because of the fire. Obviously I was curious about her, too. I figured maybe there was something there for me, right?

I sat on a bench a few feet away from her. "Hey," I said, real casual. When she looked up, I gave her a wave and a grin. Not a quick one.

44

Logic. Okay, bro, so here's how it starts: The experience of romance is pleasurable for humans. Saba Khan is human. Therefore, we can assume that the very human Saba Khan enjoys the pleasure of romance.

So Saba said hi and then went back to her calculator.

I scooted along the bench, maybe a foot closer. "I'm Steve," I said.

Suddenly her eyes had the tiniest, flirtiest hint of an attitude. "I know who you are, *Steve*," she said.

I told her I'd seen her around, too. I wanted to tease her a little, 'cause girls can't resist that, so I asked her, "What's your name?"

She looked at me crazy, like she couldn't believe I didn't know her name. "*Should* I know your name?" I asked, all innocent.

She looked down at her homework and sort of grinned. She said something like, "Gee, guess I'm not as famous as I thought."

Finally I told her I was playing. I said, "Saba Khan, I know who you are."

That made her laugh. She lifted a hand to her dark hair and combed her fingers through it for no reason. And Dawg, her hair is super shiny.

Okay, *practice*. Here's a bit of Big Stevie history for you: I had my first date in seventh grade. I wasn't much older than you. I bought a hot cocoa for this new chick in my class, Jessica Lee, during a field trip to the planetarium. We skipped out on the "Ride the Rings of Saturn" tour, and Jessica and I got to know each other's heavenly bodies instead. That

45

was, like, six years ago. Believe me, bro, there's been *a lot* of hot cocoa in the past six years. By now I've got a reputation to live up to. And lucky Saba only benefits from this experience.

I told her I was sorry for what had happened to her family. She said thanks, and I said something like, "It totally blows," and she agreed. Then she glanced back at the school to see if anyone might be around, like, watching us.

Strategy. So this is the most important part. You want to identify the situations in which you are presented in the best possible way.

I scooted even closer. By now our knees were almost touching. "Are you gonna come to the basketball games this winter? Looks like we'll have a killer team."

She said something like, "Cool, good luck with that."

I asked her if she ever went to the games last year, and she said she didn't. She was like, "Maybe sometime, though . . ."

Now this? This was just a wee bit freaky-deaky. At Highsmith, everyone comes to the home games. I said something like, "Oh, don't you like sports?"

She closed her math book, then stretched, a *biiiigg* stretch—long arms out in front of her, clasping her hands, and she actually *rolled her eyes* a little, dude, as if she was rejecting any guilt about the matter. "I love sports, Steve. Did you go to any girls' tennis matches this year?"

I said no, and before I could even make up an excuse she leaned forward and interrupted me. "But don't you *like* sports?"

Okay, now I like girls who can tease, the ones who can give and take. I said something like, "Fair enough. How about a campus tour, then? I can give you a private tour, show you all the secret spots around here."

She was like, "Actually I'm a sophomore. If I didn't know my way around by now, I'd have to be some kind of *moron*. Don't you think?"

I stared at her, not sure if I should agree or disagree. This girl was cagey.

The wind picked up, and the leaves around us started to rattle and click. To me it sounded like a crowd cheering me on. I knew the passing bell would ring any minute.

At this point, a lot of guys would have given up, waited for the game bell to ring. But here's what I've found: When it comes to romance, just like in other areas, persistence pays off. If you don't succeed with the first strategy, try an alternative one from your playbook, right? For example, try to notice something about her that nobody else does.

My eyes took a quick physical survey, from the tip of her head to her pretty little hands resting on her notebook.

I teased her about those hands—said they were the world's tiniest hands.

She smiled again, suddenly shy, pulling her hands against her stomach like she was hiding them from me. "They're not so small."

"Here, let's compare." I held up my right hand, palm toward her. "C'mon."

She hesitated, but then she slowly lifted her left hand. She pressed it softly against mine and held it there. Her whole open hand, fingers and all, fit safely into my palm. Her eyes never left mine as we touched.

Confident. I liked that.

I said something like, "Look at that, no contest." And the truth is, bro, I was already looking ahead to a win.

On the afternoon of THURSDAY, NOVEMBER 8,
phones tucked between thighs,

STEVE DAVINSKI, SENIOR & SABA KHAN, SOPHOMORE,

discreetly exchange texts from opposite
corners of the school.

Steve:

Observation: Being w/u makes lunches taste
more delicious.

Saba:

☺ Thanks 4 the smoothie. Tart & sweet.

Saba:

(Smoothie was pretty good too.)

Steve:

Aw *blushes* Yr the smoothie

Saba:

Tmw = my treat

Steve:

Ok, so . . . 3 weeks. When u gonna let me take
u out for real? Saturday night?

Steve:
Uh . . . hello?

Saba:
Uh . . . my parents? Saturday night will never
happen. Seriously I wish. ☹

Steve:
Sunday? Daylight? Movie matinee? Lunch?
Beverage? Pretzel? Peanut? . . .

Saba:
Is offer getting smaller? Better stop you @
peanut! For now, we are limited to hanging out
after school—b4 your bball practice.

Steve:
I'll take it!

Saba:
Peanut.

JAVIER CONEJERA, SOPHOMORE,

returns to the library to write to his friend
Jennifer in Oklahoma. This time, he correctly
selects one of the regular workstations.

I promise, amiga, I will not complain about my host family today, not their house that conserves heat like a closet, not their food that contains no spices, not their TV that never, never is quiet. I wonder what complaints you wrote to your friends about my family. I know—how Pimi barks at the moon so late every night. I miss mi Pimi.

The truth is, all goes wind at the stern. I am grateful to be staying in the center of this city, not in the suburbs. I use the elevated train to go everywhere. I love the speed and the squeal of the trains, and seeing the neighborhoods passing by—so many apartment houses constructed of bricks, the color of wet sand—and in the center the skyscrapers shining under the sun like space rockets made of silver. Also, so many people! Even at my school, I admire the diversity, all the faces of the world in one classroom. I am fortunate to be here.

The best part, I have discovered a friend! The more I learn about this girl Kendra, the more I think she is incredible. You are smiling, but she is more than only beautiful. She is smart. Kendra has made a website for the auction at school. I help her with it. Every day, I arrange the donated items under lights so she can photograph them. I hold the black bed sheet for the background, and she takes the photos with her phone and posts them online.

Yesterday I had the inspiration to use white aerosol paint to make some old items look new and shiny— candlesticks, small tables, picture frames, a cage for birds. When Kendra saw, she said, "You are an artist!" I felt the heat appear on the face. I argued that I am not an artist, but she uses the items I painted as proof and tells me, "You have the eye for design. Also, I believe the artists are curious about the world—and here you are, very far from home. These things are all I need to know that you are an artist for certain."

In my life, no one tells me this before. It is true, I am curious about the world. When Kendra gives me this compliment, I feel as if the heart turns into pieces from the happiness.

Today she and I walked the hallways and asked more teachers for the donations. Kendra has a talent that is unique: She can persuade all the people to give. For example, she persuaded the teacher of dance to give free classes of yoga. She persuaded the dean of the school to give his motorcycle! To every person she meets, she asks, "Well, what do you have?" The rule of Kendra is: Every person can help. And each person follows this rule, like magic.

I want to ask her to spend a Saturday with me, so we can explore the city together. But she is more than busy, and I am shy with her. Of course, I am always shy around las chicas. Around all the people, even in this friendly city.

Instead, I asked Kendra about her friend Saba. I know this girl, too, but I do not speak with her. She is not extra friendly. She wears the long hair so that it hides the face. Moreover, after the famous fire, every person at the school knows who this girl is, and they stare all the time with eyes that are very curious, as if Saba is the thing on fire, not only her apartment.

Today Kendra told me, "Well, at first I feared that Saba would decline my idea." I fear, also, that Kendra will decline my idea of being together away from the school.

Kendra said, "Saba is predictable. I know her very well. Of all the students in this school, she is the most predictable girl! Her lunches are the same, she studies in the one place day after day. With tennis, her strategy never changes. At the practices, we all know how to beat her. She only wins when she plays the girls from the other schools, because they do not know yet how she plays."

I asked, But why would Saba respond no? And Kendra answered, "She does not like the attention. She never likes the attention."

One week after the fire, Kendra went to Saba and told her the people wanted to help her. As Kendra predicted, Saba said no. Saba did not like this idea of a big event to raise money. For Saba, this event sounded awkward to the extreme. Her family did not want the charity from the strangers. They have support that is very strong from their mosque. Also, the father of Saba is very sensitive. He feels that the family suffered alone and they will heal alone.

But Jen, my new friend Kendra knows the magic to persuade people. Therefore, we are having the auction.

"The event will be very good," I told Kendra. "No matter big or small, this event will give good things to Saba and her family."

But Kendra said, "Javier, let us not make small plans. That is not the way to think. If our plans are small, this reduces our ability to surprise the world with how powerful we can be. Yes?"

At last I was ready to speak to Kendra with the heart in the hand . . . However, before I could ask her for a date, we passed the young teacher of English, who had no donation next to her name in Kendra's notebook.

Our conversation was over—Ay de mí, just like this one. The bell rings and now I go to class.

The Spring Break will be here in four months only. I am saving the money from my paychecks to buy the ticket soon!

With love from your amigo in Chicago, whose happy fingers are sticky from white paint.

After school that same Friday,
the sky is dark by 4:30 and

ARIEL AMES,
DEPARTMENT OF ENGLISH,

carrying a zebra-striped water bottle and
a milk crate full of essays, gets a ride home from
Jean Delacroix, the art teacher.

Jean, I'll say it again: I'm going to buy a car just as soon as I make a dent on my college loans. Or a *bike,* at least. I totally should start exercising more. I spend most weekends trapped on my sofa, grading essays. If I don't watch out, I'm going to have to buy a whole new wardrobe, which, *hello,* I cannot afford anytime soon. Say, can we crank up the air in here? I'm, like, dying from carrying this milk crate. Thanks.

Hey, with all the Khan talk around school, you must feel like you're in the spotlight, too. Kind of exciting, I'll bet.

Both Saba Khan and Kendra Spoon are in my American Lit class. Did I tell you that? Sophomore honors. My favorite period of the day, and those two fit right in.

You don't know Saba? She's not like most kids. No money and no connections, I mean. You can tell her scholarship is based on her entrance test scores and absolutely nothing

56

else. Without that financial help, her parents never could have afforded the tuition.

I don't understand all the negative talk. Why would Mr. Khan—or anyone in that family—want to torch their place? Or, as the story goes, have someone else do it for them? Or cover up for someone else? It's pretty clear that the Khans are *victims* here . . . the target of some sick arsonist. Maybe even a stupid kid. That whole situation gives me nightmares. I'm telling you, the first thing I did after hearing about that fire was get some insurance for myself.

But the Khans didn't have insurance. It's not like an insurance company wrote them a check. They lost *everything*. Period. There's no financial motive. They're living in donated housing. And I mean, that family never could have predicted the students would organize this massive event to help them out. That's just luck. Kindness and luck.

And Kendra Spoon . . . You know her brother, right? Didn't you tell me he's in AP Art with you?

The funny thing is, I knew Kendra was special from the very beginning. I had a sense about her. It was something she said in class during the first week of school.

Well, every September, we read "The Lottery," by Shirley Jackson. Have you read it? One of the most famous short stories ever written. Okay, well—Jean, you should read it. I don't mean to go all English teacher on you and everything, but like *this weekend* you should read it. It's fantastic.

Every year, I read this story aloud from start to finish. It's most powerful that way. And it gets students talking.

The kids are just blown away by the ending, because it's so shocking.

Spoiler alert: At the end of the story, someone gets killed. This is not a lottery anyone *wants to win*, you understand? And afterward, every year, the students talk about how unfair it is that a member of this town has to die. It doesn't make sense. It seems ridiculous, and you feel horrified for the character who dies. The students say things like, "She should have run away." Or, "Her husband should have protected her." I've been teaching this story for a few years now, and the conversation always goes the same way. "It's not fair, it's not fair," you know? Except for this year.

We read the story, and as usual, students were shocked, and they felt bad for the person who dies at the end.

Then Kendra Spoon raised her hand. She said, "Everything you guys are saying is true. But the thing is, this woman is *not* a victim. If her name hadn't been selected, somebody else's would have. And in that case, our little *victim* would have been part of the mob. She would have participated. I can't feel too sorry for her."

Well, that shut everybody up, including me. It was the first time a student of mine ever made this point. And it's such a good one! It showed me that Kendra's an independent thinker, you know?

And, of course, in October, when the Khans lost their home, Kendra was the one who spoke up. Jean, I'm telling you, I saw it happen. Saba had been absent for a couple of days, and Kendra said, "Hey, guys, this could have happened to any of us. We need to help them." She was adamant about it. She said that if we worked hard as a community, we could even see to it that Saba's family ended up *better off* than before the fire. Isn't that something? My feeling is, Kendra didn't look at Saba as a loner or an outsider, or even as a victim. She looked at Saba and saw herself.

So no kidding, Jean, it all started in *my class*, which is pretty cool, if I do say so myself.

On the evening of TUESDAY, NOVEMBER 13,
the crumbs of leftover snacks fall carelessly
upon the open notebook of

SABA KHAN, SOPHOMORE.

Ammi sometimes teases me that my friends are imaginary. Sure, she's met some of the girls at tennis + she always asks about my lunch posse: Beti, who only eats dried fruit + whose dad travels so much for work + Danielle, with her expensive sushi packs, who wants to become a dermatologist + Kendra, the newest member, who eats anything + takes perfect notes in class + who Ammi knows about more than anyone, obviously, because Kendra is helping to lead the fundraiser. But the lunch reports aren't enough for Ammi. She complains: "You never bring your girlfriends to meet us!" It would be different if I still went to a neighborhood school. Kids travel from all over the city to get to Highsmith. My friends live too far away.

    Today, however, something new: The role of hostess was played by . . . me! Ever since we moved, I'd been dying to bring the girls here. What's the point of moving to a high-rise yuppie condo if you can't show it off?

The 4 of us came straight from school, along with Kendra's perfect notes, which we all needed to copy. My 1st quarter notes were (ahem) lost in a fire, while Beti + Danielle can always use some help in this area. Forget about my Wonder Woman haircut; Kendra is the true superhero among us, saving all of the slackers in our lunch posse.

Any deluxe tour of Park Place begins in the lobby, where the semi-cute uniformed guy whose pin says "Dom" keeps watch over everything + signs for packages. He's got it pretty easy. 9 times out of 10, he's holding a cup + saucer, sipping tea; 1 time out of 10, he's cutting into an apple with a pocketknife. (Today: cup + saucer.) I greeted him boldly by name: "Hi, Dom!" — something I never do. He smiled, but raised one eyebrow as we passed. It's always a bonus when a grown-up thinks you're up to something.

In the elevator, Kendra used her ladybug phone to take an arty selfie of the 4 of us staring up at the mirrored ceiling. She immediately texted it to all of us with the subject line, "Luxe livin, Saba style!" We stopped on 3 so I could show them the fitness center, all frosted glass + chrome, along with the tan middle-aged ladies who know each other + don't worry much about dressing modestly when they exercise. They lift with their earrings on — swag!

None of the girls asked the obvious question: "Um, can you

afford this place?" They know it's donated. (+ temporary. For how long, who knows?) Furnished corporate housing owned by the parents of a Highsmith kid I've never met. Generosity from strangers: yet another way everything changed after the fire.

We rode up to 17 + took off our shoes. Our entryway floor is a rectangle of cold white granite, like a tiny skating rink made of milk. Usually I find Salman's plastic Army men standing in rows, ready to play hockey, but not today. An excellent sign.

In fact, everything was ready for us. Samosas, chips + dried fruit, all waiting on the coffee table. The second we entered, Ammi came out of the kitchen the way a wave rushes onto a beach, like her excitement was lifting her off her feet. The woman is beyond proud of this place. When her friends call, she brags that the mother of the <u>mayor himself</u> lives in this same building. She even watches the 10 o'clock news now, just to see her new friend, "Hannah from down the hall," delivering the latest gruesome reports.

Today she welcomed my friends with the biggest smile I've seen on her in ages. Kendra had read online that it was polite to bring flowers when you visit a Pakistani home, so we'd stopped at Dominick's so she could get a bunch of bright pink lilies. Super sweet.

We were losing sunlight fast, so I opened the sliding door to the balcony. The view of the lake is the star attraction, but between our building + the water is Lincoln Park, nothing but golden trees + playing fields as far as you can see. My girls let out loud hoots of envious appreciation: success! The streetlamps lining the paths through the formal gardens had just turned on. The air was getting cold, but as usual, there was a steady parade of bikes, joggers + lots of dogs on leashes. (The yuppie dogs wear expensive puffy jackets—disturbingly like my own puffy jacket, as Salman never gets tired of telling me.)

The best part? Free tennis courts down the block. Who knows if we'll still be living here in the spring, but I invited the girls to come play with me anyway. Beti made me pinky-swear she'd be 1st. "Just as soon as it gets warm outside?" she asked, not letting go of my pinky. I promised.

Kendra took 1000 photos with her ladybug, so many that I asked if she'd be coming back to rob the place. She laughed. "I gotta ask, was your old apartment like this?"

"Like, completely the opposite."

When she turned + started taking pics of the park again, her smile was so huge, sincere, not jealous. Like she felt genuinely happy for me, which makes me like her even more.

I never invited friends to the old apartment, even though I loved it there. I didn't even mind sharing my bedroom with Salman. It was like my family's unique fingerprint could be found on every inch of space: photographs + spicy food smells, Papa's work shirts drying over the tub, Ammi's words of warning coming constantly from the kitchen. Maybe because

63

of all that, it always felt too intimate for guests to see, too private.

Meanwhile, it was a breeze to welcome the girls into my new bedroom—a space that's bigger than our old living room, with its own private bathroom + this insane showerhead as big as a personal pizza.

Beti was snooping around like a detective + she asked, kind of loudly, "What, no shrine to Steve? Where's the man-orama?"

Right away, I put my hands over her mouth + whispered that she needed to shut up about that. There is no shrine, of course, not 1 single photo. Beti may publicly worship at the Church of Boys (there exists a priceless YouTube video of her mom + aunts belting out Madonna's "Express Yourself" on a karaoke machine) but as Beti knows, that subject is off-limits here.

Instead I showed the girls my "pets"—the spiders that live in a corner outside my window. Once I asked Papa if the spiders had climbed from the sidewalk all the way up here to 17. He told me something freaky: The spiders are carried by the wind, across the water, all the way from Michigan. The buildings around here are covered with them.

Sometimes I feel like one of those spiders that have been picked up by the wind, carried for many days + dropped here, just to see the view. But on a day like today, I'm OK with it.

On FRIDAY, NOVEMBER 16, sitting in a
behemoth leather chair in the principal's office,

KENDRA SPOON, SOPHOMORE,

answers questions for an audience that includes the
principal, the school attorney, and the newspaper reporter.

Am I in trouble?

*Not at all. We just need some more information before we can let you
move forward with this whole thing. We spoke to your brother, too,
and a lot of people. So you brought in things to donate—even things
that weren't technically yours?*

Yeah, my family moves around a lot. We don't have, like,
extra stuff to give away. And we have zero experience with
fundraising. So if we wanted to contribute something, we
had to, you know, be creative. The one thing we did know is
that old junk sometimes could be valuable.

Good, and how did you know that?

On Division Street, not far from our apartment, there are
a bunch of antique shops. Everything from cheap Victorian

furniture to stacks of old magazines. You'd be amazed at what people will pay just because something's old. Get this, if you take the ugliest floor lamp from the tackiest trailer park from the 1970s, and wash it up, and put it in a shop window in a trendy neighborhood, you could probably get a hundred bucks for it. Seriously, I'm not kidding.

Wait—you donated items from antique shops?

No, from alleys! My brother said we should cruise around and see what we could find. Honestly, Kevin will come up with any excuse to get behind the wheel. He likes to drive the way other people like to breathe. He's weird about it. So we drove everywhere, from the Loop to Rogers Park. We spent whole Sundays just driving around, looking in alleys, climbing into gross dumpsters, and bringing stuff home.

So you two were driving around, hoping to find items to sell . . .

Right—plus, our mom had been *off the hook*, ranting about this auction idea, and sometimes, to be honest, we left home to get away from her and all that planning. We call her Monica the Mouth. It never stops moving.

And you guys did find some useful things for the auction.

We couldn't believe what we found! A cute wooden table and chairs, painted white, with red-stenciled flowers on the seats. We found that up in Rogers Park. Why would somebody throw them away? We found this elegant old piece of white marble, and a whole box of snow globes— totally random—and a cool, vintage ship-in-a-bottle thing. We donated it all.

And . . . well, obviously you found some artwork.

We found *tons* of paintings. People throw away a lot of art, especially, I guess, in neighborhoods where artists live, like Humboldt Park and Albany Park. Broken paintings, ripped paintings, but lots of them in good shape. I guess artists must sometimes finish a painting and not like it and not even want to *see* it anymore, so they throw it away. Or maybe it reminds them of an ex. So they throw it away. Or . . . maybe someone finds it in a closet when they move in, and they think it's ugly, so they throw it away. A lot of it, to be honest, *was* heinous. I don't mean to be rude. I am very pro artist and pro personal expression. Still, some artists must be color-blind. Not that I am prejudiced against the color-blind—

Kendra, if we may interrupt.

Sorry. I talk a lot when I'm nervous.

Don't be nervous. You're not in trouble. Where did you find . . . it?

Okay, um . . . we found *it* in a random alley, in Lincoln Park, close to DePaul's campus. In case you didn't know, college students throw out a ton of really useful stuff. But other than that, and we've said it over and over again, we can't remember which garage it was behind, or which house or building, or even which alley. We'd been everywhere. Like, I don't know, fifty different alleys.

Try, Kendra, please. Any details of that day will be helpful.

It's hard to remember specific details. All those days blend together . . . Let's see, the day was sunny . . . I mean, it was mid-October, right? So there were, like, leaves on the ground everywhere. We'd been cruising around all afternoon without much luck. We were about to give up for the day and go home. I was super hungry. I remember that! *"Food, food, food, food,"* I kept saying, because I wanted to bug Kevin to the point that he would take me somewhere for a sandwich or something. He was ignoring me. Anyway, he slowed the car when we noticed a big cardboard box, like the size you'd get a nice TV in. Not a flat-screen TV—like, old-school, *huge,* you know?

We've seen the box. Actually, we have the box.

Right, so I jumped out of the car and looked inside. It was filled with, like, books. Believe me, by now I was used to garbage. But these books smelled bad, like *boiled broccoli* bad. I would have left them. I told Kevin they stank. But he got out of the car. I was so annoyed, because I really wanted to go eat!

And?

And Kevin was like, "C'mon, some of these could be valuable." He wanted to look through them. I'm telling you, my brother sticks with things until they're done perfectly. He's thorough and super patient, just like my mom. It's a good quality in most people, I guess, but not when you're *starving* and ready to *eat your shoe* or something. So we picked up this dirty, smelly box and put it in the trunk. It weighed a ton, I remember that.

And you brought it straight to school?

No, I made Kevin take me home to eat. Actually, we left the box in the trunk of Kevin's car for a few days, because it was finals time and . . . whatever, we didn't have a chance to look through it. That's right! We were studying for exams. So that's *exactly* when we found it. The weekend before Quarter One finals. Is that helpful?

Maybe . . . So you took the box without asking anyone? You didn't knock on the door of the people who owned the house to see if—

That box was in an *alley*, with the *garbage*, and that made it fair game. The previous owners had abandoned everything inside that box, and it was ours for the taking. That's the way the world works, right? That's, like, the Law of the Alley. I mean, someone threw away that box of awesome *snow globes*, too, but nobody's asking about *those*.

True, but we're talking about something else, something valuable—

69

But nobody's claimed it, have they? Nobody called the police or the newspaper and said, "Hello, my art is missing!" You guys even put that story in the paper, but the people who called in were just nut jobs. They wanted the money—or the possibility of money—but they couldn't describe the art, or say where it came from, or say which alley they had left it in. They couldn't name any of the smelly old books it was found with. Nobody could prove ownership or show any paperwork or anything. Everybody knows that Kevin and I *found* it, fair and square. Nobody can prove anything different. You guys finally said it was ours, and so it is. That isn't up for debate. And nobody else has the right to tell us what to do with it. I feel really strongly about that.

Can I go back to class, please?

On TUESDAY, NOVEMBER 20, in a quiet art studio that stinks the way only a room that has been the scene of two weeks of carved-potato printing can stink,

JEAN DELACROIX, DEPARTMENT OF ART,

welcomes the newspaper reporter to chat for a few minutes.

It's about time, right? Yes, well, thanks for arranging to come when we could really talk. I'm glad we could do this before the Thanksgiving break, at least.

Oh, you expected a woman. Based on my email? Well, it's French. I was born here in the States, as were both my parents, but my grandparents were French. Pronounced *Jean,* "John" rather than "Gene." For example, like *Jean* Renoir or *Jean*-Luc Godard, the famous filmmakers. Or *Jean* Genet, the great author. All men.

All right, then? Moving forward. Thanks, I'm happy to talk about it. I'm eager to promote this. I'm even writing an article that I'd like to sell to *Art Forum* or *Smithsonian* or somewhere. After all, I was the first person to realize that the Spoons' "garbage art" was something special. The style of the work is unmistakable.

So here's what happened: As you may know, donated items for the fundraiser are being stored in the gym. The

Monday before Halloween, I went to drop off a box of Wedgwood dessert plates I didn't need. And like everyone else, I was browsing to see if I might bid on anything on the big day.

I should add, I *wanted* to help with the fundraiser. Kevin Spoon is in my AP Studio Art class. Kevin's not a dumb jock. He's . . . sensitive, you know? He fully engages with whatever he's doing, and that focus and commitment are inspiring to the kids around him. It's rare. As a teacher, I appreciate that.

I don't know Saba Khan, but—I mean, you've got to feel bad for that family, no matter what people are saying. I realize when there's a shortage of suspects, the default mode is usually to blame the victims, but in this case it can't be right. This wasn't negligence or a gas space heater; this was arson.

Anyway, among other items, Kevin and his sister donated eight or ten of the most god-awful paintings I have ever seen. We're talking *bad* work—sloppy composition, poor use of color—worst of all, not interesting. And along with that junk, I saw this odd, oversize album of pages bound together with ordinary string. White butcher's string that had yellowed over time. There was a cardboard cover with no decoration at all. It looked like a child's old class report that should have been thrown out decades ago. The corners of the paper were fragile, brittle, some broken.

However, on the inside, the illustrations were beautiful, a mix of heavy pencil and watercolor, these landscapes with figures, mostly girls, that you could tell had been traced, maybe from magazines. Old magazine advertisements, like from the nineteen forties. Extraordinary work.

My heart started to race and I felt dizzy. I'm not kidding, I nearly fainted. I actually took the pages and sat on the gym floor to look at them.

You haven't seen it yet? Well, it's here at school. You should go look. There are ten pages total, bound together with the string. The pages depict a coherent story—a troubling story, definitely, but coherent.

Basically, on the first page, you've got these two blond girls in flowered sundresses and they're playing in a park. The girls have a big ball, like a beach ball, with stripes and rows of stars. The park is lush, intensely green, with these gigantic flowers and a few odd creatures: enormous butterflies, a yellow dog with orange horns, a snake with the head of a little pink kitten . . . The details are surreal, you understand? No, not like Dr. Seuss. It's darker, more textured, very much the style of an earlier era.

Then you turn the page, and five men appear. They look almost like Civil War soldiers, wearing gray uniforms and amusing gray caps with feathers. They have serious faces, angry dark eyes, and they carry rifles.

Turn the page again, and there's a battle between these two groups. It's extremely violent—pages of gruesomeness. The girls stripped naked, wounded, bloody stuff. A few more girls come to the rescue and join in. The final pages are filled with gray explosions and brilliant, vivid fire. In the end, this delicate girl army somehow manages to defeat the five soldiers. The girls stand victorious on top of the lifeless pile of men, and they all hold hands in a circle—I mean, like some bizarre Brownie troop.

To me, this was immediately identifiable as the work of Henry Darger, a Chicago artist who died in the early nineteen seventies. The fascinating thing about Darger is that he lived and worked in complete isolation. He was a hermit. If you saw him on the street, you might have thought he was homeless.

He worked menial jobs his whole life—janitor, dishwasher—and lived alone in a cheap rented apartment in Lincoln Park. In fact, probably not far from where the Spoons found the box of books. Darger never sold any art during his lifetime, or even tried to. It wasn't until after he died that his landlord discovered what Darger had left behind. His very modest living space was filled with this obsessive writing and brilliant artwork. And just like that, Darger's unique vision was revealed to the world. It's one of the great stories of twentieth-century art.

Oh, and one other thing. In this series of images, once the girls are unclothed—how shall I put this?—well, it's no longer clear they're *girls*, anatomically speaking. For me, this sealed the deal. Gender ambiguity: classic Darger.

Sitting there on the gym floor, I realized I was holding a potential art treasure.

First thing I did, I got to my feet and called the principal to the gym. I showed her the paintings and told her what I suspected. Dr. Stickman looked through the album slowly, her nose a bit wrinkled. The pages are really *dirty*. Not pornographic, of course, but dirty as in *grimy* after decades of dust, soot, and neglect. God only knows where they've been these past seventy or eighty years. *Not* displayed. The colors are as bright as the day they were painted.

When I told Dr. Stickman that the album might be worth an enormous sum of money, her whole expression changed. I saw her eyebrows lift slightly and—off the record?—I could tell those gears were working. Her lips crept into a smile, and she wanted to know how *much* money I guessed it would fetch "at a real auction." I told her I honestly didn't know.

Next, the two of us called those Spoon kids to the gym. We had to find out where this artwork had come from. But the kids both seemed doubtful.

"*That* is worth something?" Kevin asked. "Those watercolors?"

"The naked girls?" Kendra said. "With the little, uh, *things?*"

Regina was clutching the album, white knuckles and everything, so I said something like, "Kids, this money could change your lives."

"But I mean, there's no signature anywhere," Kevin said, still not believing. "Is there a name on any of the pages?"

"There wouldn't be," I told him. "Darger didn't sign his work, because he didn't expect anyone to see it. He was an extremely private guy."

Finally Kendra Spoon seemed to get it. Her face broke into this huge smile and she said, "But this is amazing! If this artwork really is valuable, and we sell it . . . think how much money we'll make for the Khans!"

Unbelievable, right? She was still thinking of the *Khans*. Remarkable generosity.

I should be clear: I am not an art historian and I'm

certainly no Darger expert. But I've seen his work in galleries many times. The art community in Chicago really worships him. And once you've seen that work—I mean, you cannot forget it. Seeing Darger's work is like getting a vivid, specific look into the subconscious mind of this other person, a look into Darger's own *dreams*.

I'll say it again, I'm not an expert. Actually, my field is fiber arts. Look, those are mine, hanging on the wall there. Thanks. No, I don't like that term. "Quilt maker." To me, it sounds feminine, rural, and unsophisticated. Please, I am a male fiber artist, I work with textiles, and I live in the city.

And let me tell you something, between you and me. I'm not altruistic like the Spoons. I should have kept my mouth shut and let this Darger work go unnoticed in the gym. I could have waited a month or so, bid on the piece at the auction, and probably gotten it for ten bucks. Then I could have sold it myself and moved to Paris . . . where, trust me, there are plenty of other men named *Jean*. Forget teaching watercolor technique and papier-mâché to a roomful of distracted teenagers. I could be working full-time as an artist. That's been my dream my whole life. Here I had an easy opportunity to make that happen, and I blew it.

Listen, if you ever get tired of the newspaper business, you could write a damn good book about my life. Maybe call it Portrait of an Idiot.

That same day, arriving early at the gym before
basketball practice,

STEVE DAVINSKI, SENIOR,

discovers the newspaper reporter sitting in the bleachers,
waiting for Kevin Spoon.

Whoa, whoa, whoa—you're a newspaper reporter? Let's hold up a second here, sir. I am president of the senior class. Nice to meet you. Maybe you should be talking to *me* about all this, okay? I'll be happy to give you a few minutes. You got your recorder turned on?

The thing about me is . . . I mean, I know a lot about a lot of things, but if there's one thing I don't know *squat* about, it's art.

However, I do know something about investing. My dad works at a bank in Skokie. Investment advice, retirement planning, that sort of thing. He tells me how crazy markets can be. And of all the crazy markets, the craziest one of all is the art market. Insane.

Seriously, I wish my parents had dropped a few grand into this guy Darger back in the eighties, when you could find his work in the local galleries. They were affordable then. These days, his art goes for, like, eighty to a hundred

grand each. Or more! These paintings of little girls and
butterflies and soldiers. *Eighty to a hundred grand!*

Anyway, as you know, what Kevin and his sister found
was not one Darger drawing, but a whole book. Ten pages.

Here's some basic math for you: Ten times eighty grand
equals eight hundred grand. Right? A truckload of cash.
Except that since these pages are all bound together and tell
a story, they're worth more than that. In this case, the album is probably worth more than the sum of the individual
paintings.

My first guess, the art was worth a million, at least. Had
to be.

The art itself? To be honest . . . I think it's kid stuff, and
more than a little creepy. I mean, the violence in the pictures doesn't bother me—it's no different than what you see
in video games. But whatever, girly watercolor paintings
aren't my thing. For me, the interesting part is the financial
value.

So on Halloween, out of the blue, I saw my dad standing outside the main office here at school. This isn't so
unusual, because he's on the board of directors. He's their
financial guy, so he comes for meetings a lot. I went over to
say howdy, and then saw Kevin and Kendra Spoon standing
there, along with Mr. Delacroix, the art teacher. I ended up
following them all into the principal's office.

As you may know, walking into the principal's office is
like walking into the Oval Office. Oil paintings, brass desk
set, everything's got a shine to it—including the principal

herself. I mean, she wears those dark suits and do-not-mess-with-me shoes, like someone who doesn't shy away from a fight. That's just who she is.

Dr. Stickman made some introductions, and then we all sat down in those fancy leather chairs. The hilarious thing was, I had no business being in there. I should have been in class! At the same time, I don't like to miss out on what's going on, you know? I usually go where stuff is happening. Plus, I get pulled out all the time for student-government shenanigans. So I sat down and listened.

The first thing out of Dad's mouth was to the Spoons. He wanted to speak to their parents. Kendra said he could call her mom whenever he wanted. She wrote down the phone number and handed it to him. "Before you call, you'll want to clear your schedule," Kendra warned him. "Mom loves to talk."

Kevin just laughed.

Anyway, Dad told the Spoons he wanted them to get this artwork appraised and insured. He started getting into the details, the hows and whys, making notes for Kevin and his sister to take with them.

Only thing is, the Spoons looked at the grown-ups as if they were nuts.

Mr. Delacroix was pacing the room. He said something like, "Listen to what he's telling you, kids. I haven't slept a wink in two nights."

Kevin cleared his throat and was like, "Thanks, but we're not interested in insuring the artwork."

Nobody said anything, which was completely awkward. Kendra finally said, "The thing is . . . well, we *donated* it to the school fundraiser."

"That's correct!" Principal Stickman said. "The girl is absolutely right. It was a donation to the school fundraiser. If anyone should insure it now, it should be the *school*." She sat back in her chair and folded her arms. She wasn't happy, that was obvious.

My dad looked at the Spoons the way he looks at me when I ask to borrow his good car. "You're saying you still want to sell the work and give the money to the Indian family?"

"Pakistan," Kendra corrected him. "Saba's parents are from Pakistan."

Dad shrugged, but I could see he was embarrassed.

Mr. Delacroix said, "Kids, right now, it doesn't really matter what you plan to do with the artwork, exactly. Think for a second. People are going to know about this thing. Before long, *everyone* is going to know. That means you have to protect it."

Dad was like, "What if it gets stolen? What if there's another fire? You'd lose everything. Get an insurance policy, even for a month or two, so you sleep at night."

The Spoons were not into it. They said they didn't want the hassle, or the attention, when the artwork was going to be sold so soon anyway. "Besides," said Kevin, "*we* wouldn't lose anything. It's just something we found in an alley. It doesn't have any real value to us."

"But it might bring in some money for the Khans," Kendra added.

"Then get it insured for them," I said suddenly, thinking of Saba. Everybody turned and looked at me, like I had farted or something. "Seriously, guys," I said, "please do it for Saba. Protect the art for her sake."

Kevin and Kendra stared at each other, and even though neither of them said anything, I could see some freaky *telepathic* sibling communication going on. After a few seconds, they both had these tiny smiles, and Kevin was nodding, and I thought: *Score!* I'd convinced them. That felt awesome. It made me glad I'd crashed this little meeting.

Then Dad gave us a quick intro to the insurance business. He told us that when it comes to art and antiques, the insurance value on a painting is worth even *more* than the auction value. It's different for cars and ordinary stuff. To replace a car is the cost of the car. Simple. But to replace something rare or unique, like art, it's really impossible.

"Who will pay to have it insured?" Principal Stickman said. "An insurance company won't insure it for free. Now if the art belonged to the *school*, couldn't we—?" She looked to my dad for support, and he was like, "Of course, the board would be happy to insure it. It wouldn't be expensive to buy a policy for a month or two. I can call my pal Brian over at—"

"Our mom will pay," Kendra Spoon said. "It will be her donation to the auction."

Kevin nodded and said we should call her right then.

"Let's not get ahead of ourselves," Mr. Delacroix said. "We need to have this work authenticated before we can even talk about insurance."

A couple days later, on Friday, an appraiser came to school. Apparently she's a top dog in the field. This chick was *eccentric*, which is a polite way of saying she was weird. All dressed in black. Pink scarf tied around her neck, covering half her chin. And she had on these clunky round glasses, which I guess passes for *chic* these days. We were all crowding her, asking questions, so she took the album into the principal's office and spent about thirty minutes alone with it. We could see her through the office window, photographing the pages, scribbling in her notebook. When she came out, this goofy art lady seemed almost excited. She said a few words to the effect that they really might be authentic. She asked Principal Stickman for permission to take the album with her, so her lab technicians could do some chemical testing.

Plus, she said, she needed to show it to other people. Because, even if the work could be authenticated, which would be awesome, they had to determine what *class* of Darger's work it belonged to. Even artists have off-days, I guess, so their work gets ranked in quality. Top level, second level, third level, and so on. And that ranking, within the artist's body of work, helps to determine the value.

Principal Stickman was standing in the corner, hands behind her back and looking down at the floor. Between you and me, sir, you could tell she was pissed at the world. She muttered something like, "It seems you will have to ask the Spoons for permission to take them with you."

Next to me, Kevin was like, "Totally fine with us. Take whatever you need to see if any of it's worth something."

A couple weeks later, the appraiser lady came back with the paintings and a signed appraisal—which I assume you have seen—along with the excellent news.

APPRAISAL CORRESPONDENCE

MEMO

Date:	**November 16**
To:	**Ms. Monica Spoon**
Cc:	**Regina Stickman, Highsmith School**
From:	**Louise Denison**
	International Fine Art Authentication &
	Appraisals
	Chicago, Illinois

I am very grateful for the opportunity to appraise this work.

Based on the distinct style, the age of the materials, and the unique subject matter, this was easy for me to recognize as the work of Henry Darger—probably made between 1935–1945. I could take this work to any number of reputable galleries in Chicago, and they would say the same thing. In fact, I did show it around to confirm that what I was seeing was real.

There is a difference, of course, between *recognizing* the work of a particular artist and *authenticating* it. The process of authenticating art can take quite a long time. There are many fascinating stories of an art gallery—or an art scholar—spending years working to prove the authenticity of a piece of work, tracking down evidence, identifying correspondence or journals or gallery sales records in which the piece is referenced or mentioned. All these details come together to create what is called the artwork's "narrative," or provenance—the story of how it was created and what has happened to it since then.

Authenticating work by Henry Darger is challenging, because the paper trail is, at best, incomplete. He didn't attend art school, didn't exhibit or sell his work, didn't trade or even correspond with friends. The ideal situation would be to establish that this work was part of the collection found by Darger's landlord upon his death in 1973. That body of work has been extensively catalogued. I regret that these ten watercolors are not part of it. If they were, their value would increase substantially.

However, as with any artist whose work is emerging, when you consider that there were many years before Darger's work was discovered and appreciated, things did "go missing." Items got thrown away. Darger himself may have discarded this album of pictures. It happens more often than you might think. And if/when a piece of this art later reappears, we rely upon the judgment of the community of appraisers to see if it's "right." In this case, two young people who have demonstrated little to gain (by authenticity or lack of authenticity) found this volume—the right watercolors in the right condition—in the right neighborhood in the right city. The unique story of their discovery will now become part of the provenance of this particular work. It's a narrative that Darger collectors will trust. And many of them would be happy to own this collection, despite knowing the uncertainty of its path to the present day.

Darger was meticulous about labeling his illustrations. Typically we see hand-printed, penciled notes on his work. He has not written anything on these pages. Possibly these are rudimentary sketches—ideas for something he was planning to do on a larger scale—and that will affect its value to collectors, too.

At this time, however, we are pleased to confirm with a high degree of confidence that this is authentic, second-level work by Henry Darger (1892–1973). A conservative estimate of the value of the collection would be $350,000–$450,000. Of course, at a well-advertised auction, it could sell for much more. Insurance value: $550,000.

I have attached the necessary paperwork, which should remain with this work going forward.

Congratulations, and thank you again for the privilege of seeing and appraising this important work.

STEVE DAVINSKI, SENIOR,

continues his conversation with the reporter.

Okay, so I was off by half a million. Still, five hundred fifty K is a major stack of coin, am I right?

At that point, the Spoons took out an insurance policy on the artwork, and the album got locked up tight in the gym office. This helped us all to breathe a little easier, you know? Knowing everything was safe. My dad was happy. Mr. Delacroix was happy.

The only freaky part is, the Spoons still want to donate the artwork to the auction. It's unbelievable. People are saying, "Are you effing nuts? You can't donate this thing. That money can change your life!"

And Kevin's like, "But the whole point was to raise money for the Khans. Maybe it sounds crazy, but it's what we're going to do."

At practice the other day, I heard Coach P telling Kevin, "You have college tuition ahead, a house to buy someday. Trust me, kid, it's one thing to be generous, and it's another to be a moron." Kevin really respects the coach, but even she couldn't convince him.

Kevin's attitude is that his family is financially comfortable. He feels "fortunate." All I've heard is that Mr. Spoon, whoever he was, has been dead a while. He left the kids with a trust fund. I'm thinking college costs are taken care of, you know? And so they're sticking to this plan to use the Darger money to help the Khans. At one point, Principal Stickman posted a letter on the school's website. Did you see that? Here, I'll pull it up:

[He grabs an electronic tablet from his gym bag so he can show the Web page to the reporter.]

To: Principal Stickman
Subject: Artwork donation

A message to the Highsmith community:

(Dr. Stickman, please feel free to share this. We have received many, *many* thoughtful phone calls like yours.)

With all of you, we celebrate this unexpected good fortune. We do appreciate your guidance about how to proceed on this matter. However, at this time I respectfully submit to the wisdom of my children, Kevin and Kendra. After all, they are the ones who found the treasure in the first place. If they have decided to sell the Darger artwork and use the money for the benefit of the Khan family, then I support that decision. The Khans are part of our community, and something that benefits one family benefits all of us.

Most of all, I admire my children's altruistic spirit, which gives us hope for the future of the great nation called the United States of America.

Sincerely,
Monica Spoon

That's the kind of people they are, these Spoons. I guess that particular flavor of crazy runs in the family.

All I know is, my girlfriend, Saba, is suddenly worth half a million dollars.

*Afterward, as the gym floor swarms
with his teammates running drills,*

KEVIN SPOON, SENIOR,

finally gets a chance to speak to the reporter again.

You know what's funny? I meant to tell you this the other day. My sister and I first learned about Louise Denison in *your* paper. This was last summer, long before we had any clue we might need her help. But the story really caught our attention because this woman's life sounded freaking awesome.

Do you remember the article? Ms. Denison has an "eye for art," the story said, an "expert genius," "glamorous globetrotter," passionate advocate of self-taught artists who work in isolation. "Outsider artists," the article called them, "whose work often isn't discovered until after the artist is dead." The article said that Denison had just returned from India, where she had seen the work of a guy named Nek Chand, an ordinary government worker who spent half his life building this elaborate, whimsical kingdom in the woods near his house. Twenty-five acres, thousands of sculptures, gods, people, animals, made of cement, marbles, bottle tops, broken glass and tile, you name it. And the cool part was, he did it all in secret.

When Mom showed us the clipping, she told us, "Here's the perfect job for one of you." The newspaper story included a big photo: two cement people, bug-eyed, straight nosed and long necked, covered head to toe in shiny beads. And dozens more just like them in the background.

I said, "Mom, do you want me to build you a secret kingdom in the woods?"

She was like, "No! Look, the art appraiser. She lives in Chicago, but she travels all around the globe, scoping out amazing art. And she gets paid for it. Who wouldn't want to do *that*?" She stuck the clipping on the fridge, between an article about a lady who designs super-tiny houses for rich people and one about the dude in Taiwan who invented Razor scooters.

So earlier this month, when we needed to have the Darger artwork authenticated, we were all like, *yes!* We knew exactly who to call.

My sister nearly flipped when she finally got to meet Ms. Denison. Kendra was all, "I gotta be honest. I want your life."

"I want your *luck*," Denison said. "You found this in an alley?"

After she authenticated the work, Denison told us that when a painting is not part of the artist's known body of work, then the painting usually doesn't have a title. Since this art was legit, she said, Kendra and I had the right to name it. Our book of Darger watercolors definitely needed a title before we auctioned it. I mean, to me, "Untitled" is about as interesting as a car without tires.

Kendra suggested something creepy like *Naked Girls Fight Off Old Men*. She said it would generate a lot of interest from the general public.

"But wait, are they *girls*?" I asked. "A certain part of their anatomy says otherwise."

With a choking sound, Kendra indicated we had reached a place beyond her comfort zone. Mom said, "Now listen for a minute. The gender ambiguity doesn't suggest that Darger was a pervert. Just the opposite. The research suggests he was truly an *innocent*. It's possible this profoundly isolated man did not know there was a difference between boys and girls."

Anyway, best way to put it was, the gender of the kids in the album was dubious.

Mr. Delacroix had shown us a list of Darger's titles. A lot of them don't make sense. Things like *At Jenny Richie*. Or *At Jenny Richie at Hard fury/2000 Feet Below*. Or *Sacred Heart: Battle of Marcocino*. The titles don't exactly roll off the tongue.

Darger also wrote a 15,000-page illustrated novel he called *The Story of the Vivian Girls, in What Is Known as the Realms of the Unreal, of the Glandeco-Angelinian War Storm, Caused by the Child Slave Rebellion*.

I mean . . . right?

Our mom knows way more about art than we do. She was an art major in college. No matter where we've lived, she's always taken us to museums and taught us about artists. Mom deserves the credit for coming up with the title we used: *Dubious Figures Frolic in a Fantastical Dreamscape*.

The best part is thinking about what the money will mean to the Khans. They already moved into a new place. Picture it: This family goes from living in a cramped apartment in a so-so neighborhood to a Lincoln Park penthouse with marble floors and a sweeping view of Lake Michigan.

Kendra and I started this thing, and it's snowballing. Everybody is on board to transform this family's life for the better. And the Darger artwork . . . obviously, that's the key. We never could have expected that. It's like a magic rabbit yanked out of a hat.

To be honest, it still blows my mind that I am one of the people who got this going. For the rest of my life, no matter what else I do, I can tell myself: *How cool that you pulled that off. You changed that family's life.*

Wait, sorry. That sounds self-centered. Your story isn't about us. Put it this way, maybe your story can be about what happens when people come together to help each other. Even people who don't really know each other. It's the power of teamwork, right?

Speaking of which, I should probably get onto the court. Otherwise, Coach P is gonna have me running drills until I puke.

Editorial:
True art of people
helping people

HIGH SCHOOL fundraisers typically don't make the news. After all, schools routinely plan events to help pay for sports programs, classroom computers, even music equipment.

But the upcoming charity auction at the Highsmith School on Chicago's Near North Side has made plenty of headlines this month. Among the items up for sale is a booklet of drawings by Chicago "outsider artist" Henry Darger (1892–1973). As numerous media sources have reported, the artwork was found in a discarded box left beside trash cans in a Lincoln Park alleyway. The drawings, which were authenticated this week, have been appraised at more than half a million dollars.

Darger's posthumous reputation among collectors is "one of the great stories of 20th-century art," according to Mr. Jean Delacroix, an art teacher at Highsmith.

The discovery has brought welcome public attention to a fundraiser that is more remarkable for a completely different reason: All the money raised will go to one specific student. Not to extracurricular activities, not to infrastructure, but to the family of one sophomore girl who recently lost her home in a fire.

Sensitive to privacy issues, Highsmith officials asked that the student's name not be made public at this time. Besides, as Dr. Regina Stickman, the school's principal of nearly twenty-five years, told a reporter, "One family's tragic fire is not the story. The real story here is the inspiring response to the fire."

Dr. Stickman stressed that students, not administration, are leading the effort. "What's happening this month says something important about our school culture," she said. "Our curriculum is designed to make ordinary students into extraordinary citizens—and we are succeeding!"

"We want to help," said Kevin Spoon, a senior basketball player who has helped to organize the effort. "It's the power of teamwork, right?"

His sister, Kendra, agreed. "This family needs help. We can make this story turn out okay."

These Highsmith students deserve an A+. The Darger artwork may add a splash of colorful glamour to this fundraiser, but we should not lose sight of the bigger story: the simple, shining example of caring young people at Highsmith who came to the aid of a peer.

In a society that focuses too much on results and outcomes, it's easy to get distracted by celebrity names and out-of-the-blue financial windfalls.

This Thanksgiving weekend, we give thanks for good intentions.

For those of us at the *Tribune* who are proud Highsmith alums—and there are quite a few—this act of altruism renews our faith that the sacred honor of Highsmith students still burns bright.

The auction is planned for Saturday, December 15. For information about bidding or donating, visit the Highsmith School website or contact the school directly.

Chicago Tribune, **November 25**

Late on FRIDAY, NOVEMBER 30,
curled up on a bed that feels several sizes too big,

SABA KHAN, SOPHOMORE,

stares out the window at the vast, black lake.

I've already gotten used to this million-dollar view. For a while, it made the obstacles in my life seem almost manageable. But on a snowy night like tonight, I can't see anything in the distance but darkness + ice. Maybe the lake will be beautiful in summer, but it looks scary now, miserable + cold.

When we 1st heard all the talk about an "art treasure" at school, I didn't believe the paintings could be meant for my family to keep, or sell. I figured whoever owned them before would want them back—or the Spoons would want to keep them for themselves. But that didn't happen. Ammi + Papa tell me not to worry about it or question it. "It's God's plan," they say.

Is that so? Does that apply to everything? Because evidently it was also God's plan to provide me with my own personal <u>hottie giant</u> who hangs around my locker + sends flirty texts + carries my empty tray to the nasty conveyer

belt after lunch. (Psst, I owe you 1, God.) If Ammi + Papa
knew about Steve + me, they would not jump on board
with God's plan. They would freak. Ammi wants to manage
my life the way she manages her kitchen. She says, "You will
understand, baby, someday."

But I don't understand. Just like she wouldn't understand.

I didn't even see the Darger watercolors until after I
learned they were valuable. Someone had decided the artwork
should be locked up safely until the auction, so they moved the
album into the gym office, along with the theater club sound
equipment, cash boxes from basketball games + the popcorn
machine. Usually I like being in the gym office, any chance to
visit the big can of tennis rackets Coach P keeps for us. I
always check that my lucky pink Wilson hybrid is tucked in the
back, waiting for spring. Waiting just for me.

Coach P put the Darger album on an easel, borrowed
from the art annex. Mr. Delacroix added a box of rubber gloves
so that any visitor who had gotten permission could look
through the album without damaging it.

The first time I went, I expected the pictures to be
the prettiest thing I ever saw. The pictures were not
pretty. Maybe there was something sweet about the girls,
how carefree they seemed at the beginning. The setting was
dreamlike + beautiful, like illustrations from a children's book.

But the fighting + the violence were shocking. I wouldn't
want Salman to see it.

97

As soon as I saw the paintings, I wished we could sell them as quickly as possible. Auction them as a set, or individually, it didn't matter. We would use the money to invest in my family's dreams + turn something traumatic into something good. Best of all, we would take control of our lives again—not sit waiting, like pathetic spiders on a window ledge, for the wind to come along + carry us somewhere new.

Every few days, I went back to the gym to look at the paintings. Each time I looked at those strange, violent images, I had 2 distinct thoughts: 1) I will never, ever understand the art world; + 2) this ugly story was the story of my beautiful future.

Then today everything changed. The moment I entered the gym, Coach P stopped me—literally stood in my way + blocked me from entering the office. She put her heavy arms around me. At 1st I thought she was only going through another of her bizarre crying fits. I've gotten used to it. "I'm so, so sorry, hon," she said, pulling me close.

"I'm feeling OK today, Coach," I said. "Really."

"Gone," she whispered into my ear. "All gone now."

I felt smothered in the colossal expanse of her boobs. I had to crane my head back, away from her, in order to breathe. "Things are being replaced," I said. "We have what we need. Don't worry."

"Saba, no," she said, taking me by the shoulders. "Listen to me now. I am talking about the art."

98

When I asked her what she meant, she let out a mournful little squeal, like air released slowly from the pinched mouth of a balloon. I couldn't imagine what she was talking about.

"Someone . . . or some ones . . ." she said gently. "They took it."

I pushed her arms away + ran into the office to see the easel for myself. It was empty.

Coach P followed me, saying, "It must have happened during one of the PE sections today. And now it's gone . . . gone . . . gone." The balloon began its slow sad squeal again.

I reached for the edge of her desk to steady myself. I didn't know if I could make my feet move forward, 1 step at a time, out of that office. My hands slowly searched my body for my phone. I needed to talk to Steve, or Beti, or Kendra. Anyone. I wondered if the school had called Ammi + Papa yet.

Gone—gone—gone.

The ordinary hallway suddenly seemed dangerous to me, full of strangers. My eyes scanned the passing faces, searching for—what? How was I supposed to know what the face of a thief looked like?

All at once, I stopped dreaming impossible dreams for my family + instead I began to pray. The shift was automatic, a comfort.

Maybe this is what Ammi + Papa mean by "God's plan." When someone else's dream conflicts with my dream, God decides whose dream wins. I haven't stopped praying since.

99

ACT II

FAROOQ KHAN, U.S. CITIZEN,

Yes, of course, I understand why you must interrogate me about this theft. Sit down, please. I will tell you all I know.

For me, yesterday was a very long day at the factory. Boss shouting nonsense from his stool. Plus, the snow-storm—thick snow that trapped all the cars in their parking spots—this made the driving difficult. When I finally got home, my wife, Khawla, told me that I should let neither work nor snow affect my mood. Easy for her. She does not deal with snow when she does not want to. I do not like when my wife tells me how to feel.

Even before I removed my coat, the phone rang. I answered, and when I heard the voice of the principal from the school, I was not pleased.

Detective, I will tell you something: I do not enjoy this woman. After the fire, when the school contacted us about offering this temporary residence, Principal Stickman had stressed what a "fortunate opportunity" it would be for us to stay here. How "lucky" we were—"people like you," she said—to be able to live in these luxurious accommodations. "But only temporarily," she stressed, again and again.

I feel "lucky" when I do not have to deal with people like this woman, the way Khawla does not have to deal with snow.

Still, I am a respectful man, you understand? I said, "Good evening, Dr. Stickman. How may I help you?"

She said, "This is *not* a good evening, I am afraid." This woman's tone was so stern, so scolding, that I first wondered if perhaps Saba had misbehaved in a class.

"What has happened?" I asked, and she told me plainly that the school had lost the Darger artwork. Or, not *lost* it, she made that clear—but it was missing. She told me, "It seems to have been removed from the gymnasium some-time this afternoon."

"Removed," I repeated.

"Taken. *Gone*," she said, without purpose. "Naturally, we asked Wendy Pinch, our PE teacher, but she assures us that she did not see anyone remove the Darger album from the gymnasium."

Detective, I felt such a shock. I let my eyes roam all around the kitchen, resting there at the gas stove, then climbing up to the ceiling molding, over to that elegant pendant light fixture, and then across the room to my wife's concerned face, which surely mirrored mine.

"This is a mystery," I told the principal.

She said, "Coach Pinch claims she did not see *anyone*

looking at the artwork today. This is unusual, because, as you know, the art has generated a good amount of interest."

I listened, letting the gravity of this news settle in my mind.

The principal said, very slowly, as if I were mentally impaired, "Mr. Khan, if we do not have the artwork, we cannot sell it at a big auction."

"This seems logical," I said. "Without this artwork, there would be no need for a *big* auction at all."

"Exactly," she said. "Of course, as soon as we have recovered the artwork, we may proceed with the event."

I wondered, was this woman suggesting that I, or someone in my family, had taken the artwork? As if we were *imbeciles* who were too impatient to wait for it to be sold? Did she expect me now to return the artwork so the "big auction" could proceed?

To be polite, I simply agreed that yes, we looked forward to the return of the artwork, too, and the auction. I believed it was time to end the conversation.

Instead, this woman told me, "Mr. Khan, as you know, many people in our community have worked together to help you and your family in your time of need. We've all sacrificed."

"And we are grateful to you," I said, allowing this lie to escape my lips. I reminded her that the efforts had led to some very positive publicity for the school, and she admitted that it had. I said, "So it seems that everybody wins. . . ."

"Precisely," she said. "And isn't that nice?"

"Until now," I added.

"Mr. Khan, this community has gone beyond the call of duty to help. Moving forward, I hope you will judge us based on the remarkable generosity of our intentions, rather than on today's unfortunate turn of events . . . which, you must admit, hardly could have been expected."

"Hardly," I said. "I trust you will contact us with better news soon."

We ended the call.

My wife stood at the countertop, preparing chicken curry and biryani rice. She stirred the food and said, without emotion, "The artwork is gone."

"Yes," I said.

"Stolen?" she said, looking at me.

"So it seems."

Slowly, my wife's lips spread into a confident smile. She stood straight on two feet and turned back to preparing our supper. "The police will find the person who stole it. The art will be returned. God will help us."

"God always provides," I said.

"Maybe not soon," she said, "but it will be returned. Someday. God's angels put that artwork into our lives, and it belongs to us. To our future."

I nodded, but secretly I was fearful.

Detective, to be clear, I found the very notion of the Darger pictures to be ridiculous. This is the work of a troubled mind. But God and His angels have placed this opportunity in our path, so it was clear He approves of our using this art to recover from the fire. My wife is correct. That artwork now belongs to us—to our lives, and our future.

What do you mean, God also put the fire into our lives? That is not true! The fire was *not* the work of God, but the work of the enemy of God. There are dark forces in this world, surely you know that.

We are counting on you to solve this crime. You and your men must identify the thief, or thieves, and return the art in time for the auction. If we do not sell it, we cannot remain in this apartment. On the wages I earn at the factory, I could never afford this rent. Moreover, if we go and try to rent an apartment in the old community, a landlord might learn about the fire and deny us a lease. Landlords may say my family is too much of a risk. Neighbors may complain about the potential danger.

Arson. Someone intentionally set that fire, while my family was at Saba's tennis match. We still do not understand how the fire started, or why someone would destroy our home. And if we do not understand why it happened once, how can we truthfully say it will not happen again?

America, this fabled land of opportunities. Tell me, what opportunities do we have now?

DR. REGINA STICKMAN, PRINCIPAL,

eagerly welcomes the Tribune *reporter back to
her office.*

Good morning! Thanks for coming right over. I realize you must be busy covering much more important stories.

Oh, don't worry about the silly rug. Just make yourself comfortable.

Now listen, as you cover this new development, I wanted us to touch base. While one unfortunate event has taken place on this property, we must agree that the matter is not "school related," so to speak. This is one family's private matter concerning a piece of *art.* And really I should use quotes around the word "art." Mr. Delacroix, our art teacher, may beg to differ. The whole art world may disagree, but—good, you're smiling. So we do see eye-to-eye on that matter. Not exactly something *you'd* like to see hanging above the family room sofa either, ha!

We also agree, I hope, that the school is not responsible for what has happened. That can't be your story angle.

This problem does not concern academics or curriculum, nor is it in any way reflective of my administration. In this case—which is not really a *case*, of course—the school is merely the setting. The school is not a criminal. I mean, for goodness sake, when a bank gets robbed, the police don't run off and arrest the mayor, do they?

Now don't take this personally, but there is a tiny part of me that blames the media. Oh my gosh, you people sometimes blow things *way the heck* out of proportion. It happens all the time. You make lurid stereotypes out of ordinary students. Ordinary *average* students, if you want to know the truth.

The heroic Kevin and Kendra, the S'wonderful Spoons! And the poor Khans, the calamitous Khans, "born under a bad star." How ridiculous to conclude that some people are heroes and others victims—that it's ever that simple.

Besides, this is no longer a story about one or two students, or one family. This theft affects us all, the whole community. We're all victims now.

Hey, maybe that's your headline.

But is it even possible for you, or for anyone from the outside, to fully understand why things have happened as they have, when we struggle with the basic questions ourselves?

Let me tell you something. I am sometimes required to make difficult phone calls to parents. It is one of the least pleasant duties of my position. Cheating, plagiarism, fighting, these cases cross my desk all too often. In fact, take a look at this.

*[She removes a leather-bound tome, the size
of a telephone book, from a shelf.]*

This manual provides guidelines for administrators to
use when making such calls. Look, I mean, it's unintention-
ally hilarious; one chapter includes actual *telephone scripts* to
follow when sharing unpleasant news with parents.

There is, of course, no script in this whole book to use
when telling an immigrant father, whose home has been
lost in a fire, that valuable artwork, which is to be sold at
auction to benefit him and his family, has gone missing.

Exactly. None of these scripts are even close!

I shouldn't laugh. The call to the Khans was awful to
make. I was delivering news that held dire consequences for
every member of that family. As gently as I could, using
my own words, I explained the situation. I needed him to
understand, to alter his own expectations about what the
future now promised. I told him, "Mr. Khan, if we do not
have the artwork, we cannot sell it at a big auction."

To be honest, this Khan man was very rude and quite
short. As if he blamed me! Who can say what causes people
to behave they way they do?

But listen, I don't wish those Khans any ill will what-
soever. And let me stress something else. No one is more
determined than I am to recover that stolen artwork. After
all, I have a personal interest in seeing those Darger paintings sold at the school auction.

You see, when we hired the auctioneers, we wrote a
special contract. As their fee, the auctioneers will take ten

percent of the gross sales. Standard practice. It requires a lot of time to prepare an auction and to pay the auctioneer. These people are professionals, especially the ones you want for an event of this caliber, and they deserve to be compensated for their hard work and expertise.

Also standard: As compensation to the school for hosting the event, we will take ten percent, too. Yes, *standard*—just as we take a percentage of proceeds from school plays and basketball games. After all, if we need to open the school on a Saturday in December, that means paying for utilities and security, et cetera. Come look at my utility bills sometime. You'll see why we can't give anything away for free.

In this case, if the paintings fetched what the expert predicted, that might get me—more accurately, might get the school—well, about fifty or sixty thousand dollars, at least.

Mind you, the Khans still stand to gain eighty percent of the money raised at the auction. Not bad, considering . . . I mean, to be frank, Mr. Khan did not find the art, he was not storing the art, he didn't insure the art. As far as I know, he hasn't even *seen* the art! That's a cozy deal, if you ask me.

But without the art? Well, there is no benefit to losing it, if that's what you're hinting at. What could any of us gain from that?

For all of us, it is essential to recover those paintings before the big day. That's not even two weeks away. We have placed this matter into the capable hands of our city's law enforcement.

That same morning, having announced she is
"too upset" to go to school,

SABA KHAN, SOPHOMORE,

reaches for her notebook in an attempt
to manage her anxiety.

Guess what? Your old buddy, the SW, just called. She actually asked me what was "top of mind." Seriously, what does she think is top of mind? Top, bottom + middle, too. Oh man + <u>that</u>, my 70-page, college-ruled friend, is just one of the many reasons there was no way I was going to school today.

For starters (+ maybe you don't know this, you being a notebook), on mornings like today, the wind off Lake Michigan will burn your skin off if you're not careful. Is it possible that, over generations, locals don't even feel it anymore? My boy Steve can walk around Chicago on the coldest days without a hat or coat. Just a big hooded sweatshirt, that's all he needs.

Meanwhile, me? I wear a donated coat. Huge, puffy—metallic blue. It makes me look like a VW Beetle. But when I'm standing at the bus stop on cold mornings, I don't mind at all, because I'm a warm VW Beetle.

Even in that toasty coat, I could not face going to school today. I'm not ready for another round (quite so soon) of stares from everyone there. Stares of pity + curiosity + suspicion. Thanks, but no. I can only handle pitying stares from people who actually know me.

Yesterday I lied—the biggest lie that ever came out of my mouth. I told Ammi + Papa that I was meeting up with a study group. For once, they didn't ask questions. They have worries of their own. Maybe they were relieved that I was able to focus on schoolwork at all.

A block away from our high-rise, Steve was waiting next to his car, wearing nothing heavier than that goofy sweatshirt. It was way too cold to talk outside, so we jumped in the car to escape the wind.

I should pause to clarify (in case disaster strikes + Ammi ever finds this) (*shudders*), nothing physical is going on between Steve + me. Nothing _could_ go on. I have zero interest in fooling around with Steve + less than zero interest in marrying him. Obviously I want to marry a Muslim. But that's a long way off, after college. In the meantime, what? No attention from boys, no companionship? While I'm not proud of lying, I see nothing wrong with chastely spending time with a flirty male classmate if/when the opportunity presents itself.

Still, as we buckled our seatbelts, I was suddenly + intensely aware of being alone in the car with Steve,

113

unsupervised. I never would have attempted this in the old neighborhood, where people would leap, in a giddy wolf pack, to the wrong conclusion. It didn't matter that there was so often a difference between what something looked like + what something truly was. What mattered was how the thing looked. On this street, no one would ever recognize or judge me, but that didn't make the situation feel any more normal.

Maybe this anxiety was written on my face, because the 1st thing Steve suggested was that we get my mind off the robbery by doing "something far, far away from your real life."

I said that sounded perfect + he said, "OK . . . Art Institute?"

I thought he was joking, so I was like, "Sure, why not?" Before I knew it, we were speeding down Lake Shore Drive toward the museum. How perfectly <u>insane</u> to visit a place filled with valuable art, when the 1 piece of valuable art that might have changed my own life has been jacked. It wasn't until we arrived at Millennium Park, at the entrance to the museum parking garage, that I lifted my hands in protest: "Stop!" No way was I going in. Among other things, it was too risky, too public.

He said there was this "awesome little spot" he knew inside.

I was like, "Steve, <u>seriously</u>. No, no, no."

There is something irresistible about a boy who is flexible + open to suggestions. Steve made a U-turn + then we were driving north on Michigan Avenue toward anywhere. We passed all the glassy expensive stores near Water Tower. Despite the demonic wind, the sidewalks were jammed with tourists carrying holiday shopping bags. We reached the park at North Avenue + Steve turned west, away from the lake, + continued all the way through Old Town. When we drove by the gates of Highsmith's campus, I closed my eyes for a few seconds, hoping maybe I could block that negative drama from my thoughts if I didn't actually look at it.

Sitting like that, with my eyes shut, the distinct aroma of Steve's car made itself apparent. Cheap maple syrup, eggs, sausage. I asked him: "So what's with the fragrance in here? Did you eat breakfast in the car before you picked me up?"

He got this adorable, embarrassed smile. "No . . ."

"Weird," I said. "I swear someone's been chowing down in here."

"Well, I mean, I do stop at Mickey D's most mornings during the week, before school. Or sometimes after practice . . . Whenever I see a drive-thru, really, that's an excellent clue for me to grab something."

So then I was teasing him + he got all defensive, laughing. "What can I say? Look at me. A guy my size needs to eat!"

I told him something hot to drink sounded pretty good to _me_ right then + he nodded. "Whatever you want," he said. Which was exactly what I wanted to hear.

He drove farther west + we finally stopped in a

115

neighborhood I didn't know at all. A mix of old brick
warehouses, grungy thrift shops with metal security doors
+ some trendy newer places too. Steve parked + fed the
meter. We found a diner that was decorated in a neon-retro
style, blue plastic upholstery in the booths, the Beach Boys
harmonizing on the jukebox. Hideous, but warm.

The place was empty. Steve ordered at the counter. I slid
into a booth in the back + slipped out of my puffy coat.
1 minute later, Steve joined me with the drinks: hot tea served
old-style, vintage cups + saucers. He sat next to me. I have
to admit, sitting so close to him felt good, safe. The boy is
all leg, his thighs like planks of wood covered in denim. Steve
is the only person at school who makes me feel protected
without also making me feel like a victim.

He put his arm around me, a bit shyly. I told him it was fine.
Then he stroked my hair a little, told me it felt like silk.
He said, "Sorry, I just wanted to see what it felt like."

"It's OK," I said. It did feel nice to have his fingers
touching my hair. Surprisingly, it didn't feel awkward. It felt
tender, respectful.

Steve whispered, "You were right. This is way better than
looking at some old paintings in the museum."

The tea, along with his body so close, helped me warm up,
but my thoughts wandered a bit. As much as I like being with
Steve, a part of me wanted to be out knocking on doors,
picking up clues, searching for a thief.

Pushing his hand away from my hair, I told him that there was one important thing I needed to know + I didn't want him making jokes.

Listening, he took a deep breath. He jumped out of the booth, slid into the opposite seat, facing me. He looked distressed. Then he said, all serious: "Saba, I'm not a virgin. I'm sorry if that bothers you."

OMFG. I nearly died. My face must have turned 30 shades of red. I managed to suppress a whoop of laughter + was like, "Whoa boy, that's . . . that's very interesting, thanks. But that's not it."

He exhaled, as if the subject had been weighing on his mind.

I told him to answer me honestly. "Do you think I stole the paintings? Or my parents did?"

His face expressed nothing but shock. "Of course not! Saba, you're my friend. I mean, you're becoming more than just a friend, in case I haven't been crystal clear."

"A lot of people must think we took them."

He said it wasn't true, but I insisted it was. As my words spilled out, I nearly began to cry. "People still think we set the stupid fire ourselves!" I said.

He was so sweet, grabbing my hands. "Where is this coming from? I'm sorry, but you're talking crazy. That doesn't make sense."

"It totally does! Look at us, we benefitted from the fire. New condo, new clothes. New lives . . ."

117

Steve said we couldn't have known what would happen. He said, "The auction, the donations, that was all other people, not you. People want to help you. It feels good to help other people."

I tried to describe my fear that everybody would be judging us — for benefitting from the fire. I worry about backlash. I said to him, "Don't tell me you haven't heard people talking."

He was quiet for a moment, a trace of sadness creeping into his eyes + I knew I was right.

"Saba, I believe you. Isn't that what matters?"

He was right. It mattered to me, almost more than anything.

To a lot of people, Steve may seem like an arrogant, doofus jock, the kind of guy who only cares about himself. Maybe even I thought so, at first. + yeah, not much earlier, that doofus jock _had_ wanted to take me to the art museum. But I know he cares about me. At that moment in the diner, sitting on opposite sides of that booth, all I could think was: This guy's on _my_ side. People can surprise you.

We finished the tea, but neither of us was ready to go home. I dropped some tip money on the table + we left. We started down the block, but it was too cold to wander outside, so we ducked into the 1st open storefront we passed. It was a massive Goodwill store, packed with merchandise. It was so cold in there that the guy working the register was wearing a coat. The air smelled foul, a combination of leather + sweat, like the inside of an old lady's shoe. It must be rank in summer. The floors were dirty + the aisles were tight to navigate. Holding hands, Steve + I passed a mountain of stiff, twisted purses, racks + racks of awful clothes + enough furniture to fill a dozen apartments. It took me a few seconds to recognize the irony: This was only a bigger, sadder version of all the donated stuff in the school gym. The store made me feel crabby. I might have insisted we leave, but it was freezing outside + at least Steve and I were together.

"Actually, not all of this is terrible," he said. "Maybe your family could use some of this."

"Steve, that's not the way to solve my problem, OK? We don't want some stranger's dead grandmother's useless junk." Why was I barking at him? Not attractive.

We kept wandering. There were boxes of ancient paper from one of the local mills, white butcher paper turned yellow + a long wall of used books, most of them 50¢. In one corner, we found a pile of old film magazines. I flipped through an issue. Movie stars from the 1940s, posing in swimsuits like some hot stuff. One of the ads featured a little girl with cute blonde curls. The girl sat with her elbows on the kitchen table, + watched her mother decorate a cake. Staring at the ad, I realized I'd seen that innocent face before.

For once, Steve seemed to read my mind. "Hey," he said, all playful, "in case the artwork isn't found, do you want me to draw some pictures for you? If I traced this, it would look just like a Henry Darger."

"No, it wouldn't," I said. "But someone else could, maybe."

"I'll show you, if I tried really hard to imitate it—"

"I don't <u>want</u> any fake artwork. I don't even want the <u>real</u> Darger stuff. I only want to <u>sell</u> them so my family can finally get a break." I closed the magazine + tossed it back into the pile. I felt generally angry, but it wasn't fair to take it out on Steve.

I was like, "Dude, I should warn you. I might be going crazy. We need to figure out who jacked that artwork."

His smile was so confident. "We will! We have 2 whole weeks."

That wasn't exactly true, I realized, and the thought cheered me. The school event may be in just under 2 weeks, but even if the art is found after that, we can still sell it. Even if it turns up 6 months from now.

Steve said, "The art will be found. I promise. I will help you."

I leaned into his chest, letting his heavy plank-arms surround me. "Thank you for saying that. I know you mean it + it makes me feel better."

2 seconds later, I wriggled out of the embrace. I didn't want to tease Steve, or mislead him. Plus, I don't care who you are or how bad you feel: No one wants to hug a boy in a depressing thrift store that stinks like an old lady's shoe.

STEVE DAVINSKI, SENIOR,

I'm telling you punks, she didn't take the art. I don't want to hear that again. The girl is innocent. End of story.

Guys, listen, I've been with girls for a lot of reasons. Each girl, a new reason, you know? Sometimes it's the way a girl looks. Sometimes it's crunch time in the semester and I need help with homework. Once, I'm not proud to admit, I dated a girl because her dad had some very sweet Cubs season tickets.

And who are we kidding? Girls date me for reasons of their own, too.

My mom, she's really into this New Age stuff, right? She says that every relationship between two human beings has a *purpose*. Every relationship teaches us something valuable. Guess what? I'm big into learning! I plan to be a lifelong learner.

High fives—right, guys? *Yeee-esssss.*

You know, sometimes the reason is mysterious to me,

too. Sometimes I don't know why I'm dating a girl until after I get to know her. That's how it was with Saba at first. Maybe I felt sorry for her, you know? Maybe I wanted to protect her.

It pisses me off that some of you guys think Saba's family is up to something. That they're lying. Guilty of arson. Guilty of bilking the entire community of money and donations. Last week I actually heard some dude in the locker room talking about "immigrants coming in and scamming us." Is that what this is about? I mean, what the hell?

If I believed what people are saying, it would change everything. No way would I give her my time, my reputation. I've got no time for people who don't play fair.

I've spent my whole life playing by the goddamn rules. Other people's rules, sure. But they're the rules that determine who gets to be a success in life. Maybe they go something like this:

Rule 1:   Be nice to people.
Rule 2:   Study hard and get good grades.
Rule 3:   Don't curse in front of grown-ups.
Rule 4:   Try to win in sports, but think positive
           even if you lose.
Rule 5:   Obey any other rules people come up with.

That's all I've ever needed to worry about, right? With these rules, I get to be popular, to win. Anyone can win, if they follow the rules. But it turns out that Saba—she's got a whole extra set of rules. Sort of like:

Rule 6:   Fit in with two cultures.

Rule 7:   Speak two languages fluently.

Rule 8:   Have two separate wardrobes.

Rule 9:   Ignore the prejudice surrounding you.

Rule 10:   Try to look innocent.

How would you like that? Sound easy to you?

Yesterday afternoon, I came to school for the open gym. After steaming up my car windows for a couple of hours with my girl, I needed a good workout, you got me? Yeah, a couple of you dawgs know what I'm talking about. So I'm here yesterday, running some drills, and suddenly Coach is yelling at me out of nowhere. "Where *are* you today, Davinski?"

In four years, the only useful thing I've learned from Coach P is how to keep my mouth shut.

Thing is, she was right. My mind wasn't on my game. Free throws bouncing out. With Coach P, three misses for any varsity player, during practice or otherwise, is grounds for fifty push-ups. I missed three in a row. No kidding, this mess with Saba's family has really got to me.

Fortunately Coach wasn't on *her game* either. I saw her over near the gym office. She was spinning around, looking like she lost her favorite pair of tube socks or something. So I skipped the push-ups.

Do I really believe my girl? I want to. I need to. But how can I ever know for sure until we get our hands on that art again?

That's where you punks come in. Starting today, you guys are like my army, right? You're my eyes and ears.

You're gonna help me turn this place upside-down until we find that freaky artwork. We will assume that everyone at Highsmith is guilty until proven innocent. You come to me immediately if you find anything that looks weird or might be useful, okay?

And hey, whoever finds it, I promise you *I will make it worth your while.* Your life will change around here. You won't even know what hit you.

Concurrently, in the gym office,

WENDY PINCH, DEPARTMENT OF PHYSICAL EDUCATION,

pours a lukewarm cup of joe for the police detective.

I know what people are saying: "The artwork was stored in the gym. Wendy's in charge of the gym. If the art went missing— heck, let's all blame Wendy!"

All weekend, people have been looking at me funny, like I was the one who took it. Nobody has flat-out accused me, but see, now you're here questioning me about it. Nothing against you. In fact, it's kind of refreshing to have somebody come right out and ask.

You and me, we're practically in the same business. We both deal with the little turds of the world. And believe me, after thirty years, I know cons. I know all the tricks, scams, schemes, frauds, and dupes. I know the new ones, using the fancy gadgets to share answers. I know the old standards, like the one about the dropped test. Jesus, I love the dropped test. You're not familiar?

"Coach P, Suzie must have accidentally dropped her answer sheet on the floor. I picked it up on my way up here."

Yeah, honey. *Sure* Suzie dropped her answer sheet on the floor. Suzie accidentally dropped her answer sheet on *your desk* so you could accidentally copy *her answers*—you know what I mean? Classic.

And how about an ugly bruised ankle to get out of gym class? "Coach P, I can't play basketball today. See, my ankle is bruised." Listen, I'm not shy about rubbing eye shadow off any kid's ankle, just like that. Heck, I *invented* the blue-eye-shadow bruise!

I'm telling you, scams? I kinda love 'em. God's honest truth, teachers live for this stuff. You should hear us in the staff lounge.

But this robbery? There's no pleasure in this.

Meanwhile, my boss, Regina, keeps stopping by the gym on a regular basis just to scratch her little chin and "think about where it could have gone." *Yeah, let's keep thinking about it, honey bun.*

I do take some responsibility, of course. I must have seen *something.* I'm not a teacher who bounces from room to room, know what I mean? It's not exactly convenient to play dodge ball in the computer lab. I'm here in the gym all day, every day. And detective, I do not take my eye off the ball.

I spent the whole weekend going over it in my mind, trying to remember anything at all—anything unusual. Friday was a regular schedule, and that means basketball, kickball, kickball, kickball, strength training, kickball, kickball, basketball. The way I work my schedule, see, every day of the week is different. However, all Mondays are the same, all Tuesdays are the same, and so on. I have to do it that way or I'd lose my marbles.

Fridays, like I say, are kickball heavy. Kickball requires the whole gym. We'd been playing most of the day, one group after the next. Mid-afternoon, I realized the artwork was gone. Not even a cloud of smoke!

Why would I take it? Me, ordinary, churchgoing Wendy Pinch. What would a normal person like me do with a piece of artwork like that? Not exactly my taste, know what I mean? Darger's stuff doesn't really belong on my coffee table, between *Michael Jordan: Modern-Day Michelangelo* and my big book of Audubon birds.

What, sell it on eBay? The criminal underground, yeah, that's maybe more like it. But honest to God, I don't meet a lot of those guys in my line of work. Stuck here in the gym, I don't often see those fat cats in pinstripes, running their crime syndicates. Shocking to you, I'm sure.

You're asking who I think took it?

[She hesitates, removing invisible bits of lint from the sleeve of her Highsmith Athletics sweatshirt, which is the color of tomato soup.]

See, to me, the answer is obvious. I don't want to name names, but think about it. Life is about strengths and weaknesses. Every day I watch kids pick up weights that are too heavy for them to lift. The squirts think they can do it. But they can't. They call out for help. "Spotter!" So, after years of watching this, I began to see the same thing happening *outside* the gym: people, everywhere, who try to lift more than they are, in fact, capable of lifting.

My feeling is, when people lift too much, they panic, and then they get desperate. But in real life, people don't call for a spot. They cheat. Cheat on tests that are too hard, cheat on taxes, cheat on marriages. They commit crimes. You weren't born yesterday. You know what I'm talking about.

Listen, who do we know who's in over her head? Who has the responsibility for a large, expensive operation but doesn't understand the first thing about budgets? Who's been saying for the past three years that she doesn't have money for salary increases, yet still manages to redecorate her office every year? The kids don't even complain about being sent to the principal's office anymore. They say, *"Au revoir, mes amis. I'm off to Versailles!"*

Who complains about the teachers' "excessive" use of copy paper and dry-erase markers? Meanwhile, she only goes to education conventions when they're held in places like Florida or Hawaii.

Who needs the money most because enrollment is in the toilet?

Final score: Who is the most desperate?

Not naming names, see, just asking questions.

Years ago, I wrote a confidential letter to the board of directors. These are the top dogs, right? The people who make the decisions about our administration. I told them what I was seeing, all my concerns. I didn't have much experience under my belt, but I knew right from wrong. My parents raised me that way, see? I made a list of the sketchy practices and unfair policies that I was seeing. Nothing personal, just facts. I spent a couple of days on it, typed it out, and put it in an envelope. Never sent it.

I was afraid for my job, you know?

Two years ago, I pulled my cowardly head out of the sand and wrote another letter to the board. Same circus, different clowns. Spent a week on it—but never sent it. I needed this job.

But listen, I found out recently I'll be coming into some money in a few months. An inheritance from an aunt I hardly knew. Gal named Muriel, wife of my dad's brother. A complete and unexpected windfall. It means I'll be able to retire at the end of this school year.

No more student scams. No more administrative shenanigans.

Anyway, because of this inheritance, I feel a lot freer to speak up when it comes to the administration.

Somebody needs to say *something*. You understand what I'm getting at?

JAVIER CONEJERA, SOPHOMORE,

writes once again to his friend Jennifer in Oklahoma.
Next to him, the coiled, cast-iron radiator hisses and spits.

On the phone I told you about this crime at school, but I could not tell you that my host family is very strange concerning it. The Davinskis enjoy the mystery programs on the TV—murders for all the nights of the week. This family has become police detectives in their minds. Last night during the meal, they spoke about the crime at school, one suspect after the next, like bites of the meatloaf on the forks.

Mrs. Davinski is certain the thief could not be the principal, because the person who stole this artwork required a partner. Someone to monitor the hallway, to distract. She said, "Who would help the principal like this? She cannot find someone to be the 'Secret Santa' for her during Christmas!"

Jen, this family uses voices with a volume that is unusual, as if they are speaking through the long cylinders. Possibly because of their height. A family of giants, not only Steve. Because of the size of these people, the furniture in the house is too large for the rooms. The rooms feel cramped and noisy, even in the big chicken. When I can, I escape to the backyard just to breathe, and also to smoke.

Mr. Davinski wondered if the thief is the teacher of English, Ms. Ames. He said, "She is young, smart, and the students admire her. She might be able to persuade one of them to help her. Someone to help remove the art from the building."

Mrs. Davinski added, maybe only to me, "Mr. Delacroix, more than any of them, knows the value of the paintings."

I was grateful this conversation was different from the usual: the games and the working-outs, the picking-ups and the dropping-offs. They review the schedule after supper each night, very solemn, the way my mother prays the Rosary during Lent.

Mr. Davinski said to me, "What do you think, Savior?"

Jen, my host family calls me "Savior." LOL. We all believe this is amusing, but for different reasons. It amuses them that my name is Savior and it amuses me that these people truly think my name is Savior. In September, I made efforts to correct them: My name is pronounced *Javier,* not Savior. "But it *means* 'savior,' right?" Mrs. Davinski said with impatience, as if I was banging a rock for no reason. At this point, I do not think it would be polite to correct her. "What do you think, Savior?"

Very often, when I am with my host family, my English words fly away like birds from the nest. I could not tell them how I truly think—how strange it is that no one speaks of this girl Saba and her family, nor how we might help them. How no one makes plans to go to the auction next week. I know that Steve and Saba spend time together at school, and after school, with hands that are affectionate. However, never he speaks her name at the house, except when discussing the crime.

I cleared my throat. "In my village, we say: 'When the cake is missing, you suspect the one with crumbs on the beard.' Over time, we will see the one with crumbs on the beard, and we will know the truth."

132

For once, my host family was left without words.

Most interesting to me: This family never speaks of the art. And the art is brutal! Weeks ago, like many students, I went to the gym to see this work by Henry Darger. These paintings are nothing like what I see in my country. The students around me exclaim only about the "nude girls" and the crude abuse of the children, but they misunderstand the intention of the art. These beautiful pictures tell us a story of innocence and darkness. The two aspects exist together, no? That is nature. Well, this is the truth.

After I saw the art in the gym, I wanted to see more. I wanted to know about this artist who is so original. Online I learned there is a museum in Chicago with his work. Therefore, I took the train to the Intuit museum on Milwaukee Avenue.

I remember the many museums I have visited in my life and I think of the grand structures, very impressive, perhaps with columns in front. But the Intuit museum is hidden. It is only a plain brick building with a gray metal door. I walked beyond the museum once, before I turned on my feet and located it. Moreover, the interior of the museum is quite small—only two galleries and a book shop—and modest in décor. No floors of marble, no ornamental gold frames or varnished canvases that shine under lights. At the Intuit, one sees rough wood floors, and on the walls mostly simple drawings, made by pencil, marker, watercolor. All work made by the artists they call the "outsiders."

In the back corner, behind yet another wall divider, I find another thing hidden. It is the thing that I have traveled across the city to see: an actual room from Henry Darger's apartment, made again here. Protected by a brown velvet rope, the space resembles a typical American room from the 1930s—a round table with wooden chairs, an elegant fireplace surrounded by tiles, a tall wooden cabinet. However, this room is crowded and dingy, with dark brown walls. This man Darger was a collector, a hoarder. Every centimeter of the table is piled with paints, brushes, cigar boxes filled with pencils, magazines and books for coloring; the floor is crowded with tall stacks of the *National Geographic* and the *Good Housekeeping*; near the entrance there is a container filled with many, many balls of twine; religious items dominate the fireplace mantel like an altar. According to the museum, the apartment was filled completely with newspapers, magazines and items he found on his walks. Because the things covered even Darger's own bed, he slept all the nights on a hard chair at the table.

In my mind, it is difficult to put this sad room together with the brilliant, colorful pictures I have seen. They do not appear to belong together. The following day, I went to the public library and borrowed two books about Henry Darger, so I can read more about the man. I learned this man lives his whole life with no friends, no family. As a janitor, he mops the hospital floors alone. After work, he walks the streets alone, collecting more things. Every night, he returns to his apartment alone and works on his art. Imagine this: a long life in isolation, a life without companionship.

The life of this man and the image of that room, Jen, I tell you, they sit heavy on the shoulders. During the meals, when my host family tries to solve the mystery of the theft at school, I sit in silence. I think only of Henry in that dark apartment full of clutter, drawing the pictures of the little girls, having no company but those characters on the page.

Well, I think this is a good example for me to see, no? Too many things I do alone. We have discussed this. Moving forward, I need to be more social. I must have the courage. I want to take the risks. I have traveled so far to do this—exactly for this—and I am wasting time. So now I will begin, OK?

Have faith in me, mi amiga!

Meanwhile, across the library,
sitting on a hard vinyl sofa,

KENDRA SPOON, SOPHOMORE,

speaks quietly with the police detective.

When I think about it going missing . . . No joke, last Friday I thought my head was gonna explode.

It was the last period of the day, English with Ms. Ames. My brother, Kevin, caught my attention, waving like a maniac through the little window in the classroom door. He was gesturing for me to come out to him, and I remember sitting up, like, *Seriously?* I knew something must be up because my brother and I hardly ever see each other during the day.

When I got into the hall, the first thing I noticed was that Kevin didn't look right. Ordinarily my brother is Mr. Unflappable, Mr. Easy-Breezy. I had never seen his face like this—so freaked out and full of panic. He was running the palms of his hands on his khakis like he was rubbing off sweat.

"Um, hey," he whispered, with the weakest, fakest smile I've ever seen on him.

I asked him what's up, and he goes, "So, like, the artwork is missing from the gym office. By any chance, did you take it?"

"What?" I said. "No. Why would I take it?"

We stared at each other. It seemed unbelievable. All that planning, all the work on the auction. Our reputation was, like, *on the line* because of this thing.

I kept saying, "No, no, no," and the walls around us seemed to fall away. I leaned against a locker to steady myself. If Kevin is usually Mr. Easy-Breezy, I am often Miss Rudderless Boat in a Whirlpool. That's why I'm lucky he's my brother.

He told me to chill. He was like, "Security's been searching lockers. They'll find it. Some knucklehead demo probably thought he could sell those pictures at a pawn shop." Kevin said to meet him after school in the main office.

All during that period, they kept the students in the rooms while they finished searching the lockers. No passes to anywhere, no excuse to leave for any reason. I kept waiting for Kevin to come back to my room, so he could tell me they found it and everything was okay—but he never did. After the bell rang, I went straight to the main office and found Kevin there, slowly spinning in a leather chair. He seemed as freaked out as me, which only freaked me out more. Principal Stickman told us that since the artwork "technically" was still ours, Kevin and I needed to report it stolen. Two of your guys showed up and we filled out a police report. I felt better knowing the police were around, but even then it seemed pretty hopeless.

Do I think a student took the artwork? I thought so, at

first. Everybody did. But security would have found it Friday, when they searched the lockers. Teachers have more freedom. This is a closed campus for students, but teachers can come and go. Any teacher could have moved the art to a car, or anyplace off campus. But not students—not during the day.

After school Friday, Dr. Stickman gave us her keys, and Kevin and I searched all the classrooms ourselves. I mean, it was better than doing nothing, and it felt awesome that the principal trusted us with her keys. We even searched teacher closets and supply cabinets! We found plenty of cigarette packs and bags of half-melted candy bars, lottery tickets . . . I mean, hey, whatever gets you through the day, right?

We stayed really late, climbing a million stairs and opening doors until we thought we'd pass out. Obviously, we didn't find the artwork. Whoever took it was able to walk straight out of the building with it. That's something only a grown-up could do.

I hate to suspect the teachers. I actually like most of mine.

If I had to pick one? Hmm . . . well, but any name I give you will be my opinion. Only a gut feeling, which isn't fair . . .

[Lowers voice even further.]

Okay, so in English we've been reading *The Great Gatsby*. And on the day we're talking about, the teacher, Ms. Ames, was . . . noticeably irritated with us. She had assigned the last few chapters, and a lot of us weren't connecting with the end of the book. In our defense, that "borne back ceaselessly into the past" stuff? Most fifteen-year-olds aren't exactly stuck in the past. We're thinking about this week. We're thinking about *today*.

Ms. Ames said something like, "Can't you identify with someone who was willing to do *anything* to make a secret dream come true?"

The thing is, I got what she was saying. I think of myself as a dreamer, too. But around me everybody had these bored, slow-blinking eyes, like she was talking about politics or laundry or something.

So that was when my brother showed up, pulled me into the hallway, and told me what happened to the paintings.

The reason I'm telling you this is—okay, when I was out of the room, Ms. Ames wrote a long sentence on the overhead. It's from the first page of the book: "Whenever you feel like criticizing any one . . . just remember that all the people in this world haven't had the advantages that you've had." Out of context, it seemed a little defensive. I mean, who's criticizing anyone? What advantages? I stared at that sentence for a long time.

Ms. Ames is so much younger than the rest of the faculty. Her salary is probably tiny. She doesn't seem happy at this school. Not that I think she's a dishonest person. But her point seemed to be that we're all desperate dreamers like Jay Gatsby.

I mean, the defensiveness and the timing, and her being so irritated—it all seemed weird to me. It *registered*, you know? And even now I keep wondering: What are her secret dreams? And how far would she be willing to go to make those dreams come true?

*Early that evening, while reviewing copious
notes at the station, the police detective receives a
visit from none other than*

ARIEL AMES, DEPARTMENT OF ENGLISH.

I'd like to speak with you privately, detective—if that's okay?

I suspect . . . I mean, what I know may be helpful. At the same time, I really hope it won't be. Maybe that sounds nuts.

I've worked at Highsmith for three years. My first job out of college. I always wanted to teach. I used to *play* teacher in my bedroom when I was little. My dolls and stuffed toys were my students, and I taught them about Rumpelstiltskin and the Three Little Pigs. Those were my lesson plans.

The school? I'd say it's a strange place. The campus, obviously, is gorgeous. I love the old architecture. And they spend a fortune on the gardens. Do you know who designed them? Frederick Law Olmsted Jr. Probably the most famous landscape architect of his time. He worked on the National Mall and the White House grounds in DC, the US parks system—and our very own Highsmith campus.

Plus a million other projects, but don't mention that to

Dr. Stickman. She'll tell you Highsmith was his *crowning achievement* as an artist. That woman lives in a fantasy world. Or she lives in the past, I don't know.

Sure, the gardens may look perfect, but the buildings are in sad shape. Leaks everywhere in the roof, cracks in the foundation, and broken, outdated equipment in classrooms. Think about it: If we had some security cameras in the building, maybe we could have protected those watercolor paintings.

The enrollment is down. We have too many empty classrooms. For a lot of students, the school is a family tradition. You often hear, "Dad went here, Granddad went here, Great-Granddad went here. That's why I'm *stuck* here."

That's mostly who we get. The legacies. If you look at the old black-and-white photos in the main lobby, you see the same faces we have here today. It can feel clannish at times. The kids all have names that sound like platform stops on the 'L.' "*Hello,* so nice to meet you. These are my boys, Clark and Wellington. And these are my girls, Addison, Damen, and Kimball."

Anyway, because of this dynamic, newer families like the Khans and the Spoons may have a harder time. It's not the friendliest community.

Same goes for teachers. When I first got hired, I was so excited. It turned out I was the only new teacher they hired that year. So it was a little lonely. Nobody ever took time to get to know me.

I replaced a guy named Mr. Bunder. Glen Bunder taught at Highsmith for forty years. He was a legend, and I was a twenty-two-year-old with no experience. That was a rough year.

The next year, they didn't hire any new faculty—not in any department. So I was still the "new" teacher. Same thing happened this year. No new faculty hires. Last week, I heard a teacher from the Science Department refer to me as "the new girl." After three years! And "girl"? Please.

If there's a paper jam in the copier, they blame me. If someone leaves a coffee mug on a counter in the main office, the secretary will call my classroom: "Ariel, did you forget to take your coffee mug to the kitchen again?" Meanwhile, I don't even drink coffee.

At faculty meetings, when Dr. Stickman repeats her speeches about rules and procedures, it's always "for Ariel's benefit."

My point is, if any members of the faculty want to suggest I stole the artwork . . . well, I wouldn't be surprised. I'm an easy target. I'm still the mysterious stranger in town.

But you can check the attendance: I was out of the building all morning on a field trip, and by the time I got back, the artwork was gone. For once, we can't blame "the new girl."

Besides, I don't have a car. And that book of watercolors would definitely not fit in my milk crate.

Who do I think took it? The thing to remember is, most of the dinosaurs who teach at Highsmith are too old and set in their ways to realize that a painting doesn't have to look like a Rembrandt to be valuable.

It has to be someone who would know what to do with

143

the art. It's not like fencing a TV, right? You'd need to find a way to sell it on the black market.

Well, who knows the most about art in the school?

I don't mean to point a finger at Jean. Jean Delacroix is probably the nicest guy at Highsmith. He gives me rides on bad-weather days. Generally I take the 'L' and it's not a problem, except for really cold days. Last year, on one brutally freezing day, I was desperate, so I asked Jean if he could give me a lift home. I mean, I barely knew him. But I knew we lived near each other, so I thought, Why not? What did I have to lose? Now it's a regular thing. Whenever I need a ride home, I just email him or call first. He's not much for conversation in the car. He likes NPR.

No, it's nothing romantic.

[Smiles hesitantly.]

That's funny—I mean, because Jean's gay. I don't suppose it's relevant to your investigation. He's totally out with the staff, but maybe not with the students. You know how some teenagers can be.

Jean's a wonderful artist. Did you know that? He makes these amazing quilts. Not like the quilts you see on beds, but art to hang on the wall. Incredible landscapes and portraits, things that take him months to complete. He's like a painter with cloth and a sewing machine. I always love to see what he's working on when I stop by after school to wait for a ride. His talent is really something.

Anyway . . . I hate to tell you this, but I'm going to, for

the sake of those kids. And it's God's honest truth. I'll sign anything you need me to.

As you know, we had a snowstorm on Friday. The first big snow of the season. I'd seen how bad it was getting during the field trip, but later it was even worse. Taking the 'L' sounded awful. So naturally I went to find Jean.

Even though Jean is the only art teacher at Highsmith, the art annex is massive. Like I say, the enrollment used to be bigger. There's the main studio, a sewing room, kiln, and so on. Jean's got a nice office of his own, just as big as Regina's, to be sure. And private.

Anyway, I was waiting for him, not sure where he was. There weren't any students around. I saw that Jean had some new quilt projects on a table, three or four of them, all folded neatly and stacked. I was curious. I mean, I'd looked before and Jean never seemed to mind. In fact, he always was proud of the work, glad to have someone notice his creative efforts.

I opened the first one, a late summer cornfield shown in these blazing, orange-gold colors. No kidding, I felt warmer just looking at it. I refolded the fabric and set it aside. I was about to unfold a second quilt—I actually had it in my hands—when I heard Jean's voice behind me.

He said, "Ariel, put that down."

I turned and saw him standing in the doorway. I said, "Hi, Jean! Bet you know why I'm here . . ."

He looked furious, the way he'd look at a student who was being insubordinate. He repeated, "Put that down now, please."

145

I realized the quilt I held was folded around something. At the time, I thought: *Why is there a book in this blanket?* I really thought that! I pictured an atlas. I figured it must be some technique for storing his quilts—folding them around an atlas to avoid wrinkles, or something. The funny thing is, I wouldn't have noticed anything if I hadn't picked it up.

I apologized, of course, and gently placed the folded quilt back on the pile. "I didn't mean to be nosy. It's just that I love looking at your quilt—"

"I can't give you a ride today," he told me. "You didn't call or email."

I felt horribly embarrassed. "I know!" I said. "It's just that with all the snow . . . well, I was hoping—"

And he interrupted me, sort of gruffly, and said, "Can't help you today, Ariel."

"I understand," I said. "It's fine, Jean. You're always so generous."

I was really confused. He'd never been angry with me—*moody* maybe, but not angry or unfriendly. I picked up my backpack and buttoned my coat, feeling so embarrassed. I looked out his office window at the darkness and snow. I remember thinking vaguely about my CTA fare card and where I had left it, did I have any money on me, all that.

I told him goodnight and turned for the door.

"Wait. Ariel."

I turned back. His face had softened, more like the Jean I know.

He told me, "It is awful outside. Of course I can drive you home."

I said I didn't want to be trouble. And he said, "Listen, I was going to run an errand tonight. But with the roads all snowy and slow, it will be better if I do it tomorrow. I can give you a ride."

He did give me a ride. I was so relieved and so grateful. Like I said, he's generally a thoughtful guy.

But what I never figured out was: Why was he acting so strangely?

And it was weird, because the very next day, Saturday, I was at home, doing some planning for this week. Obviously I also was thinking about all the drama at school, the Darger artwork being stolen, and how awful that situation is, in different ways, for two of the girls I teach, Saba and Kendra. I was reading *The Great Gatsby*, and—hold on a second. . . .

[She removes a copy of the novel from her bag and opens to a bookmarked page.]

I was reading, and I came to these lines about Gatsby: "He had thrown himself into it with a creative passion, adding to it all the time, decking it out with every bright feather that drifted his way. No amount of fire and freshness can challenge what a man will store up in his ghostly heart."

When I read this, detective, it seemed like a sign. I couldn't help but remember that beautiful folded quilt of

Jean's. And I wondered again what he might have been hiding inside of it.

So you see why I thought I better tell you, why I thought this information might be helpful. But like I said, I sure hope it's not.

JEAN DELACROIX,
DEPARTMENT OF ART,

*looks up from his digital camera and sees the police
detective standing in the doorway.*

Oh! You startled me!

Please, come in. Do you mind if I work while we talk?
I've got a bit of a deadline here. One of my fiber art projects
has made it to the final round of a competition. Yes, in Paris!
The award carries a prize of five thousand euros.

Well, they received the images I sent. They liked what
they saw, and now I need to send the actual piece. Before I
put it in the mail, I'm taking more photos to be safe. Honestly, I'm nervous about sending it.

It's this one.

Thanks, but the beauty is only part of why I'm proud
of it. Let's see—artists generally don't like to explain their
work, but . . . Okay, when you first look at it, it appears to be
the skyline of Chicago at night. A very detailed cityscape.

But look, try to focus only on the blue and green stitch
lines, here and here and here. You'll see that each building

contains an abstract portrait: here a painter at her easel, here a sculptor with his clay, there a writer with a book, and so on. Any city, Chicago or Paris or Des Moines, is home to many artists, all working in their solitary boxes.

Maybe our school's personal encounter with Henry Darger, the quintessential "outsider artist" in Chicago, was the lucky omen I needed for this piece to get noticed. I'm beyond excited, as you can imagine.

Speaking of Darger, how is your investigation going? Any leads?

You've got to be kidding. People are saying it's me?

That stings a bit. If you think it will help, go ahead and search my office again. Search the whole department. Open every cupboard and drawer. Leave no hand-painted meditation stone unturned. Remember, it all got searched on Friday.

While you're at it, search my house and my car. Bring in the hi-tech CSI equipment you use to examine rug fibers. The Darger album is old, crumbly. The paper is dry and brittle as a cracker. If I had transported the artwork in my car, you'd certainly find traces of it on the floor, or in the trunk.

Sorry, detective, I don't have it. Believe me, I wish I did. I've been as worried as everybody else since it disappeared.

I mean, wow—I guess I should have expected fingers would be pointed at me. After all, I'm an outsider here. I'm the one who never goes out for beers on T.G.I. Fridays with the rest of the staff. I'm the one who doesn't even pretend to care about Wendy Pinch's grandkids. I don't kiss up. I don't take sides. I don't play their office-politics games.

I learned a long time ago that there are people in this big bigoted world who won't like me, no matter how hard I try. Some people will hate me just for being who I am. Since that's true, why not just be myself? If I sound a little defensive, it's because I am.

Who do *I* think stole those paintings? I . . . I couldn't say. Unlike other people, I'm not going to be part of any witch hunt. That's your job, not mine.

[Two police officers enter the art studio.]

Wait—you're confiscating my quilts? On what grounds? Who did? A member of this faculty? A sworn statement?

[Reads the statement.]

Okay, so let me get this straight. Ariel claims that she "might have held" the artwork in this room. Didn't see the artwork, didn't see me take it, but she "had a feeling at the time." That's enough evidence to confiscate my personal property for lab testing?

I mean, I know exactly what Ariel's talking about in that statement. I asked her, very calmly, to put the quilt down because her hands were covered in blue dry-erase ink. They always are, from teaching—like Smurf hands!

I need to keep these things clean. This work is *valuable*

to me. It's not some casual hobby. Not that I expect other people to understand that, especially not Ariel. Seriously, guys, this is a woman who once asked me, "Jean, if Picasso's grandson painted a picture, would you still call it a Picasso?"

Listen, I totally get that you need a break in this case. Like I said, you can search this entire annex again. Search my car, my house, my friends' houses—I don't have it. But please, you can't just *take* those quilts. I need to send this one to Paris!

I need a lawyer. This is insane. It isn't fair. It isn't right.

Two days later, in the cafeteria, the lunch tray of

STEVE DAVINSKI, SENIOR,

lands with a clatter at the table
where the police detective is sitting.

Steve Davinski, senior class president. Right, pleasure to make your acquaintance. I've seen you around the building the past few days.

[Sits next to the detective and ignores his food.]

So it's been a bummer, you know? We never thought something like this could happen here. Feel-good story doesn't feel so good anymore, that's the thing.

If you ask me, I'd be out looking for the original owner, the guy who threw the art away. Because you know he's seen the news, and he's thinking to himself, "Hey, bonehead, why'd you leave a fortune out near your garbage cans?" Anyone would be pissed for doing that. Don't you think maybe he wanted it back? It's possible. And we know one thing for sure: *that person exists.* That unknown individual is a definite factor in this equation.

153

The problem is, the artwork wasn't locked up in Fort Knox. The gym office door gets locked at *night*, that's it. The rest of the day, it's pretty much open to anyone who's looking for a stopwatch or a herpes video.

Respectfully, sir, I'm not sure you've collared the right guy. The problem with Mr. Delacroix is . . . Listen, if you were the badass with the balls to steal that artwork, you would have grabbed it and gone, don't you think? But Mr. Delacroix remains, still explaining color theory to kids who are looking for an easy A. I mean, heck, maybe our lonely-artist guy Darger was the sane one and Delacroix's the nut.

He's gay, did you know that? Not saying it's relevant, just stating a fact.

Think of the numbers. At this school, you've got just under six hundred students, and you've got about fifty members of the staff. In other words, of our total pool of suspects, more than ninety percent are students. If you were in Vegas playing roulette, odds are you'd put your chips on the students.

So why are we looking at Mr. Delacroix or any teacher, when, based on *probability*, our thief is most likely a kid?

I realize that this scenario makes your job a lot harder. Sorry about that, sir. But let me help you out. Of these six hundred students, who can you skip? There's my girl, Saba Khan, for one. She had no motive to take the art, since her family was going to benefit anyway, by selling it at the auction.

Then there are the Spoons, Kevin and Kendra. Those guys had no motive either, since they already had possession of the art and decided to give it away. I guess, if they changed their minds or something, and wanted to keep the money, that'd be a different story. It would have been super awkward, right, if they asked for it back? But that's not what happened. They've never expressed any interest in that money. By all accounts, they've *got* some money.

So that's three people to subtract from the suspect pool. It's a start!

And if we look at who had PE that day, it makes the suspect pool smaller. I'd guess about one hundred fifty kids were in the gym that day. Coach P can probably give you her rosters.

Two minutes, tops. That'd be enough time to slip into the gym office, grab the artwork, and stuff it in a gym bag.

Isn't it true that most crimes occur because of random opportunity? Criminals spot an opportunity—an open window, a car unlocked, a fat wallet poking out of a purse—and they just *take it*.

The difference between criminals and people like us is that we may see these opportunities, but we don't act on them. People like us know right from wrong.

The way I see it, our badass, Student X, stood at the back of the gym, fielding balls for forty-five minutes. Kids are always slipping out of class to take a leak or text a friend, and Coach P is too busy blowing her whistle and running in circles to even notice. Who is Student X? That's the biggest problem to solve. In my family, we think of it as "the Davinski Code."

I can tell you one student who definitely had PE on

Friday. Javier Conejera, my "brother" from sunny Spain. This guy has been living with my family since August. Between you and me, he fits into our house like the flu.

First of all, he's essentially mute. A conversation with Javier is painful. He has zero interest in American sports—of course! He smokes cigarettes, and yeah, we're all thrilled to have six more months of that. The kid *irons* his blue jeans. At school, he spends more time socializing with the kitchen crew than with actual students. You gotta wonder what inspired him to come to this country if it wasn't to make friends with some American kids. What's he after? Our world-famous, secret recipe for tater tots?

When my family and me discuss what happened at school, Javier just stares at his dinner plate like he's gonna find the answers in the mac 'n' cheese. But I can tell you this: The dude became crazy interested in the Darger art when we all realized it was valuable. He even borrowed books about Darger from the library, using *my* card. The weird part is, ever since Friday, he hasn't said a word about it. Red flag, for sure.

Sir, I'm not saying I have the evidence to prove Javier jacked the art. I'm only stating the facts I know. It's all valuable to you, right?

As the police detective strides toward the cafeteria exit,

KENDRA SPOON, SOPHOMORE,

steps boldly into his path and blocks him at the door.

Excuse me, sir. We spoke a few days ago? Yeah, hi. . . .

Okay, so I was sitting over at the table behind you guys, and I heard a little bit of what Steve said to you. The thing is, and I'm truly sorry for eavesdropping, but that guy is monumentally full of it, and you should know. He seriously needs to shut up. He's been talking to my friend Saba and also to my brother at basketball practice. I've heard these "updates" from both of them.

So this boy Javier borrowed a few books about Henry Darger from the library. This is breaking news?

Also relevant, in Steve's opinion: The Internet history on the family computer is suddenly filled with Darger searches, thanks to Javier's "crazy obsession" with the artist.

And oh, let's not forget, Javier is not truly part of the "Highsmith community." No long-standing, emotional ties to anyone here.

Therefore, the only logical conclusion is that standoffish, "sneaky" Javier must have taken those paintings. Because . . . why? He's greedy? He hates Americans or something? Don't you think that's a stretch? Thanks to his *host brother*, this pitiful foreign kid is the subject of a rumor that is moving around school just as fast as the craziness with Mr. Delacroix and his "criminal quilts."

I don't expect an overly confident, self-centered jock like Steve to understand a socially awkward person like Javier, a shy guy who may have a genuine curiosity about Henry Darger. But there's nothing criminal about *taking an interest in other people*, right? After all, Javier's the kind of guy who's given up a whole year of his life to come to another part of the world just to . . . you know, see what it's like! That tells you all you need to know about Javier's character. Meanwhile, I bet the only traveling Steve ever does is to basketball tournaments, where he can show a big room full of strangers—over and over again—just how good he is at his own stupid game.

Oh and by the way, Steve bragged to my brother that he already went through Javier's backpack. *And* searched his duffel bags, drawers, and closet. He came up with nothing. No stolen artwork, no smoking gun of any kind. But I guess Steve didn't think that was worth mentioning to you.

Javier told me he's gonna buy a plane ticket that will take him far away from that household at spring break. Apparently he's got one friend in this country, in Utah or

Oklahoma or somewhere. That trip cannot be coming fast enough for poor Javier.

That's all I wanted to say, sir.

Also, I apologize for the cafeteria food. You may want to call dibs on the bathroom when you get back to the precinct.

Very well, then. Thank you, sir.

JAVIER CONEJERA, SOPHOMORE,

*uses the family-room computer
to write to his friend Jennifer.*

Mi amiga, I am fortunate to have you in my life.
I describe none of these events to my mother,
because they will put too much worry in her head.
For my mother, I write only what she wants to know.
For you, I give the complete story.

The truth is, for me now the time is very difficult.
How can they believe I stole these paintings? Well, of
course because of my supposedly "brother" Steve!
Not in front of his parents, he tells the people at
school that my behavior warrants suspicion and that
my possessions should be examined. However, what
place do I have for concealing this work? The talk is
absurd. They have no proof, no motive, no reasoning.
And yet I pay for the duck!

As a detective, Steve is not in equal company as Jules Maigret or Sherlock Holmes. This morning at breakfast Steve smelled his Cheerios and said, "Son of a bee, what is up with this milk?" This slug is not capable of solving the Mystery of the Sour Milk. On Saturday, Steve returned from the basketball practice after the rest of us had eaten the meal. He exclaimed, "Why is the pizza cold already?" The Case of the Cold Pizza—this is another challenge for Inspector Steve.

For this reason, Steve's theories do not molest me. However, the students pass this idea from mouth to mouth, like a virus. The students spoke very little to me from my arrival. But now it is worse.

For example, in the hallway next to my locker, there is a large H on the floor, the color of blood. It is rude to step on this H and the students give the effort to avoid it when they walk. In the past, sometimes I get a little bump from the rushing student who sees only the sacred H and not the sacred me standing at my locker. Possibly this is normal. However, now every day the students are giving me the bumps, with full intention, as they step to avoid the H. This is also rude, no? They will make me crazy.

Well, there remains in my locker the white aerosol paint for the auction. Maybe tomorrow I will spray the faces of all students who give me the bump. This will teach the lesson, jaja! ☺

Also very strange, my boss in the cafeteria gives me no smiles now. She tells me she does not need my work after we return from winter break. So now I need to find another job. Perhaps away from the school is better for me.

Only my friend Kendra remains sympathetic. Today when she sat with me in the library, she offered to review my essay on THE GREAT GATSBY. My face must have revealed the surprise that she was willing to give help, because she whispered, "Steve Davinski is an imbecile. I know you did not steal the art."

I gave thanks for the trust, but she waved my words away with a hand. She tells me, "I do not know you, so I cannot trust you. No offense, but what will you do with it? It would be difficult for a Chicago citizen to know how to sell it. Who would you call?"

Exactly! Who would I call? I have no one here! She said, "This crime going on. It makes the behavior of the people very strange. I want to tell you that

Americans are not bad. Americans are helpful and friendly."

The truth is, Jen, the people here are friendly to me like they were the day I arrived, nothing more. The friendship with the Davinskis has passed by its date, like the milk in the chicken. "You must visit my country," I say to Kendra, "to meet the people you describe."

She reviewed my essay and she tells me it is very good. Then I give her a confession: I wrote this essay last year, when I was a freshman. I needed only to translate the words for this class now.

Kendra expressed surprise that we read THE GREAT GATSBY in España, and I said, "Of course, for school. EL GRAN GATSBY. We read many important American novels. My favorite is REBELDES."

She stared, and so I attempted to translate the title: "Rebels?" This is the very famous American book, no? About the group of friends who find so much trouble always. However, Kendra does not know it.

I asked her if American students read DON QUIXOTE DE LA MANCHA, and she made a frown. She said,

"Not at any school I ever attended." I could not believe it. This is one of the most important novels in history! Not only for España. Kendra said she knows Don Quixote, but not the book. She hid the face with the hands, but peeked through the fingers. "I apologize. We suck."

"Only some of you," I said. And then I tell her all about my host family. How they call me "Savior." And they use no spices. I am starving for an onion!

Kendra said there is an excellent tapas place near her apartment and gave the promise we will go together. For the first occasion in many days, my heart felt light.

Of course, this happiness did not last. Soon after I saw Kendra, there was more bad news, this time concerning the two books I borrowed about Henry Darger from the library.

First I discovered them missing from my backpack. I thought, well, maybe it is possible I left them at the house. I did not worry. However, soon after, I found these books outside the doors of the school, soaking in the snow! At the same time, I saw some boys from the basketball team. They were staring, as if

164

they had waited for me to come outside and discover this damage.

I told them to go fry asparagus, but Jen, I felt more despair than anger. Why am I the outcast for no reason? The cold silence is one thing, I can ignore that. But I cannot ignore the damage to these books. These are expensive art books! I will be required to pay the library an eye from the face. This takes from the money I save to visit you.

The spring break needs to come as rapidly as possible.

Tomorrow I will go to the school library and ask for the famous novel REBELDES. The author is a teenager named S. E. Hinton. I want to spend time with these friends again.

On THURSDAY, DECEMBER 13, at 1:21 pm,

THE CITY OF CHICAGO
FIRE DEPARTMENT

closes its official investigation and files this report.

Summary of Incident: On October 1 of this year, Investigators Chau and Winter responded to 6313 N. Artesian, Chicago, at the request of Chief Holper. The dispatch time was approximately 1600 hours, arrival at the scene was fewer than ten minutes later. Investigators observed a brick construction, three-story, multi-family residential building, with smoke and fire visible in two windows on the first floor.

No death or injury reported.

The investigation revealed that fire originated near the rear of the residential unit, between the kitchen and the living room. The indicators observed and the evidence taken and analyzed revealed the

fire was started by the distribution of
a flammable accelerant and ignited by an
open flame. A tire iron was found on the
kitchen floor. Damage to the rear/kitchen
door and lock indicates unlawful entry
through the back door of the residence,
accessed by the open utility stairs.

Taken into evidence were an aluminum can,
a tire iron, a plastic lighter, and cloth
"rag" remains that indicate criminal
intent.

No criminal suspects have been identified.

Laboratory Analysis: Attempts were
made to take fingerprints from evidence
collected, but these attempts were
unsuccessful. Laboratory analysis revealed
that the flammable liquid was turpentine.

Witnesses: Residents of the unit arrived at
approximately 1730 hours, as workers were
still extinguishing the fire and securing
the property. Statements made by these
individuals testify that all members of
the residence were together and away from
the property at the time of the incident.
(Numerous witnesses subsequently provided
corroborating reports.)

During the days following the incident, neighbors were interviewed. No person or persons were observed entering or leaving the property. Nothing "unusual" was reported. The property residents are not considered suspects, nor have suspects been identified.

Property Control and Release: Department officers controlled access to the scene for a period of one week, after which the building was determined safe for repair/ re-oc, and was released to the building owner, who is not a building resident.

Statutes Violated:

IL Criminal Code

720 ILCS 5 Sec 20—1.2   Residential Arson

720 ILCS   Sec 21—1   Criminal Damage to Property

720 ILCS   Sec 21—3   Criminal Trespass to Real Property

Before school on FRIDAY, DECEMBER 14,

STEVE DAVINSKI, SENIOR &
SABA KHAN, SOPHOMORE,

eat breakfast together, in separate kitchens, via text.

Steve:
Big day tmw. How r u feeling?

Steve:
PS. I went to bed thinking about u & woke up
thinking about u.

                                       Saba:
As usual, I went to bed thinking abt the fire &
woke up thinking abt the auction.

Steve:
But in between, u dreamed abt me.

                                       Saba:
LOL, you love to think so. True fact: I never
remember dreams. Sad.

Steve:
Tragic! Esp b/c I am hilarious & handsome in
dreams.

169

Saba:

In your own dreams maybe. PS. I love that you are
always like this. Always like . . . you. ☺

Steve:

I guess, hmm . . . well, I am NEVER like . . .
Javier.

Saba:

Idea to consider: Try being nice to Javier. Unlike
you, most people do not walk into a room
assuming everybody will adore them.

Steve:

More people should try it, IMHO. Drink your
juice. See u soon.

That evening, after staying at school
for an unusual number of hours,

KEVIN SPOON, SENIOR,

calls the Tribune *reporter for a last-minute interview.*

Just checking in to say . . . well, thanks. We really appreciate all the coverage you've given to the event. My mom wanted to know if you're putting something in the morning paper, too? Every little bit helps.

Yeah, everything's ready to go. Today after basketball practice, my sister and I set up the gym. Saba Khan helped. Saba and my sister know each other pretty well, but I had met her only once before. It's got to be a weird thing for her to be going through. Not the kind of attention anybody asks for, right?

Steve Davinski stayed, too, to lend a hand. You've talked to him? I bet every school has a kid like Steve, the guy who drops into a project at the last minute and then takes as much credit as possible. I don't mean Steve's a bad guy, not at all. It's good to have someone tall like Steve for hanging signs.

We rolled out the heavy gray tarp over the gym floor,

and then set up about fifty rows of folding chairs. And sure, we were talking about what happened to the artwork. We're no different from anybody else. Saba repeated the rumor that a foreign exchange student might have taken it. That could be true. Put it this way: A person would have to be detached to do something like this, I guess. Saba was looking at Steve, as if wanting him to chime in, but he was like, "Don't get me started, I gotta live with him."

I haven't met Javier. Then again, I haven't met most people at Highsmith. But I know about the escalating cold war between him and Steve.

I could tell the finger pointing was starting to annoy my sister, so I said maybe we should leave the rounding-up-the-suspects to the police.

We set up tables at the front, then spread red and green plastic tablecloths across them. My mom gave us some fake mini Christmas trees—seven or eight of them, different sizes—that she got from a crafts supply store. We put them on the tables and plugged them in with extension cords. We had a couple fake poinsettias, too, that we put on the auctioneer's table. Mom's thinking is, if the event looks like a Christmas pageant, people will be generous and buy more things. I'm telling you, she has the whole thing mapped out in her head. She gave us notes and everything.

On the main tables, we arranged the best donations: vacation rentals, a night cruise on Lake Michigan, wine baskets, spa certificates, and lots of expensive tickets to sports games and theater. That's the stuff to mention, okay, if you put something in the paper? And off to the sides, we made room for the sadder-looking junk Kendra and I collected: used furniture, dishes, even those random paintings that may be too worthless for anyone to buy, much less steal.

Saba was looking over the items, sort of shaking her head in disbelief, like the idea was finally becoming real to her. She turned to Kendra and me with this apologetic expression and said, "It's amazing that you guys are helping my family like this. If I ever stop saying thank you, you have my permission to pinch my arms and remind me."

I didn't want Saba to feel bad or anything, and it seemed like the right time to tell her my own good news: By helping to organize this fundraiser, I found the perfect material for my college application essays. Planning this auction got me into Harvard—Early Action!

Yeah, thanks. Obviously I'm stoked about it. Dream come true, right?

So, like I explained to Saba, this project has been a win for both of us.

But then Steve Davinski muttered something sour like, "Gee, Kevin, it's completely awesome this situation is working out so well for you."

And now there was this weirdness among the four of us when nobody said anything. I stood there, like . . . *what?* Am I supposed to feel guilty for getting into Harvard? Or for saying that I did? Or for using Saba's fundraiser in my essays? I mean, give me a break. Kendra had her reasons for leading this thing, and I had mine. It's not a crime. And it's naïve to think that people go around helping people without some motivation, without expecting something in return, right? My sister and I have been working our butts off to make this thing happen. And Steve Davinski, of all people, has the nerve to criticize me for trying to take advantage of that hard work?

Sorry to get so fired up. My whole point was that Saba didn't need to feel grateful. She's not in our debt, *not at all*. That's the only reason I told her about Harvard.

Two seconds later, Saba looked at the clock and said she needed to go. Steve was only too happy to give her a lift in his car, and then Kendra and I were alone. Kendra told me to settle down, and the rest of the work went quickly. When we were done, we turned off the gym lights and went to find Dr. Stickman. The halls were deserted. It wasn't until then that I realized how hot that dang building was. My clothes were soaked with sweat, and I couldn't wait to get outside. As usual, my sister was starving.

We got to the main office, and through the glass doors we saw Dr. Stickman standing near the counter in her long wool coat.

Kendra grabbed my sleeve and was like, "Oh, snap."

I told her it was fine—staying late could be the principal's small contribution to this effort. I mean, the school has gotten some incredible publicity, thanks to you guys.

The principal straightened her back when we entered, like she'd been standing there asleep on her feet. She smiled and asked if everything was set up, and we told her it was. We finally walked out of the building into the cool air. As Dr. Stickman was activating the alarm system, she said, "Look at you both, you're sweating!"

"It's a ton of work," Kendra said, a little defensively.

Dr. Stickman said, "I know you kids must be disappointed . . ."

Before she could continue, I said something like, "Who knows? Maybe those paintings will be found someday, and we can use them for some good." I really believe that.

Dr. Stickman said to Kendra, "Your brother is quite an optimist."

"Oh, he's cheesy all right," Kendra said. I could tell the only kind of cheese she wanted at the moment was the kind with ham on a sandwich.

The principal said she would see us first thing in the morning, and she walked off toward the parking lot.

Anyway, sorry, I've been talking too long. So, like, will we see you there tomorrow? Are you sending a photographer? If you can send a photographer, that would be fantastic.

The following day, on DECEMBER 15,
after an eventful morning,

SABA KHAN, SOPHOMORE,

withdraws to her bedroom, washes her hands,
and opens her notebook.

If only there was a quick, painless way to lift the memory of this messed-up day out of my head + transfer it onto these pages . . . Then maybe I could rip up the paper, launch the stupid, sad confetti out the window + let it flutter down like toxic snow onto some poor, unsuspecting fool's head. Sorry, stranger. Tag—you're it.

If only.

Dr. Stickman asked us to arrive early this morning so Papa could sign contracts with the auctioneers + the school. When we left the lobby, Dom the doorman (cup + saucer) wished us luck. It was frrr-eezing outside. Our neighbor "Hannah from down the hall" had told us there would be cameras, so Ammi asked me to "dress up" in something traditional. Only for her, I wore my salwar kameez. I should have worn leggings under my pants, because the heat in the Ford never works. (Clueless me.)

On the ride, Salman asked where we were going. (Clueless Salman.)

Ammi told him, "Our lives changed on the day of the fire, remember, baby? Today life will change again."

"This time for the better," Papa added.

Nobody said it out loud, but we were all feeling sick that the Darger paintings hadn't been found in time. We expected that once the police had identified the thief, the artwork would be returned. They seemed so confident that the art teacher had taken it. So why didn't we have the artwork?

"In the 1st place," Papa said gently, "the art teacher should not have been teaching at the school. Men like him . . ."

This line of talk always makes me cringe. On the subject of LGBT issues, Papa's mind is stuck in reverse; nothing I say will ever shift it into forward. (Clueless Papa.) I only said, "From what I hear, Mr. Delacroix is a very good teacher."

"Saba, read your Quran," Papa said. "The subject is not ours to debate."

"All that, in God's hands!" Ammi said impatiently. "When the artwork appears again, it will be sold. We will have that money."

Next to me, Salman stared uncomfortably out the window. I described some of the items I had seen in the gym on Friday. "It'll be fun to see what people spend money on, you'll see." I tried to sound cheerful, but even I felt this intense dread. Of course I wanted the auction to be a success. But I dreaded the attention, especially the pitying looks. I didn't want people to feel sorry for us or keep labeling us victims.

I thought about that story, "The Lottery," where the townspeople choose a random person to kill — like, a sacrifice. Except this was just the opposite. My family was being singled out + rewarded, but just because of our random bad luck.

(Speaking of luck, so Kevin Spoon used my family's bad luck as his ticket into Harvard. So what? Steve was supremely pissed on my behalf + that was sweet, but I mean, you've got to hand it to Kevin. He's not relying on any dumb luck to get him where he wants to be.)

(Of course, now I wonder what led Kevin to the auction idea: a pure motivation to help my family, or a totally bogus motivation to help my family because it would get him into Harvard. I could wonder about these things for a long, long time, until my brain shattered into cold little shards, like windshield ice.)

(Moreover, I ask myself, why should one more dude going to an elite college in Boston affect my life or my plans?)

(At the same time, as much as I totally thank Kevin + Kendra, and bow down like everyone else to their charitable spirit, I want to state for the record that I would be more capable of helping my own damn self if I had access to a car, the way they do. The Spoons may be new to Chicago, but you don't see them freezing their butts off at the bus stop.

Life's different when you're rich + they're doing just fine, so—whatever.)

ANYWAY (*shaking it off*) we arrived at school about an hour before the auction + walked into the gym lobby. As usual, the air felt insanely warm, as if the thermostat was set too high.

By the strange quiet, I knew immediately: something had happened.

I looked around for Steve, but didn't find him. He'd promised he would come early + sit near us at the auction. The slacker never showed at all. So that was the 1st weird thing.

Kevin + Kendra were sitting at the raffle ticket table with a woman I didn't recognize. Maybe their mom? Kevin had his arm around Kendra, who looked upset. I wondered if they still felt awkward about what Kevin had told me about Harvard. I waved, but Kevin only shook his head sadly.

Near the gym doors, Dr. Stickman stood talking to two police officers. I wondered: Why security, with the valuable artwork still missing? People, it's a little bit late for security, I thought. (Clueless me.)

Dr. Stickman turned her head and saw us. She approached us rapidly, her expression very serious. "Mr. and Mrs. Khan," she began.

"Good morning," Papa said, shaking her hand formally.

179

"It is <u>not</u> a good morning, I'm afraid," Dr. Stickman said. "In fact, I have some unfortunate news to share with you." Beyond her, inside the gym, some activity attracted my attention. Dr. Stickman drew a breath: "We have located the Darger artwork. What I mean to say is, the art has resurfaced . . ."

I suddenly felt too giddy to listen to her story. Slipping past Dr. Stickman, I rushed into the gym to see what had happened.

<u>Thank you, God!</u> I thought.

10 or more policemen stood in a group, halfway down the main aisle. Surrounding the artwork, I thought. Having the brains to protect it this time. One of them was taking photographs. I wedged myself between 2 of the men so I could see it again. Then my eyes seemed to play a trick on me.

The paintings lay in a pile on the floor. Each page of the album had been ripped out + torn into strips, leaving these hideous shredded scraps. As if that wasn't enough, 3 big sections were <u>burned</u>, black wet patches of ash. It appeared that some fool had deliberately set the areas on fire, then came to his senses + doused them with water.

The smell was intense. I reached up to protect my nose + mouth. I stared for many seconds, not believing. This was like a bad dream, more surreal than Darger's original images. Among the ashes, I saw glimpses of things I remembered: pale sky, orange fire, a soldier's black gun, the soiled hem of a little girl's yellow sundress.

Why would someone destroy the paintings on purpose? It seems so cruel. I understand why someone would steal the album, either to keep or sell—but this? No one will benefit from this.

It makes no sense. It makes <u>zero</u> sense.

This important art discovery—destroyed. All that money—gone. My family's biggest dreams—lost.

+ for what? <u>What</u> is the <u>point</u>?

As long as I'm asking all the unanswerable questions: If I stare at my phone long enough, will Steve ever call me back today? Where is that boy?

ACT III

On THURSDAY, DECEMBER 20,
while on break at the shampoo factory,

FAROOQ KHAN, U.S. CITIZEN,

receives a visit from an insurance investigator. Mr. Khan
removes his wire-framed eyeglasses before speaking.

It is good that a claim has been submitted. I understand why you must investigate. An investigation will reveal the truth, as it did when it excused my family completely in the matter of our fire. We place our trust in the system to do what is right. I will tell you everything I remember about Saturday.

The reappearance of the artwork, in that form, was very stressful for my family. The police photographed the scene many times, examined the area for evidence. They used all the minutes we had before the auction.

There is no question, I think, that these destroyed paintings are the same paintings that were stolen three weeks ago. I never saw these pictures, but several teachers and students confirmed they are the same.

Just before they let the people in for the auction, the police carefully removed the artwork, scooping up the remains with gloved hands and taking them to a police van.

Then many hundreds of people entered the room. They

must have been waiting in line, outside in the cold. They brought the cold air in with them. The chairs filled, row by row. In the end, many people had to stand in their coats. A gymnasium filled with coats.

The auctioneer was a short man in his seventies, wearing a pale-blue cowboy hat. He did not look like a man who has ever been to a cattle ranch. My wife wears less gold jewelry than this cowboy. But his voice was strong, clear, and he worked fast.

During the bidding, my family and I sat in front. I expected the auctioneer or the principal—someone—to invite me up to the microphone to say a few words, to acknowledge my thanks. I had prepared a few lines to this end. However, no one asked me to speak.

Ordinarily, I might have felt foolish. All this public scrutiny could make anyone feel odd. Given the newest circumstances, however, we felt only numb. The sad reality overtook me like nausea. *The paintings—destroyed.* So the auction would not change our lives forever with the sale of an art treasure. The money collected only would help us to get back onto our feet again.

At best, we would return to where we were before the fire: in a safe, small apartment, with rent paid by this job. I reminded myself to be grateful, to give thanks to God. This modest success, after all, was the intention of the efforts from the beginning.

Across the gym, I saw our new landlord, Mr. Musgrove, standing with his wife. I had met them only once before, when they came by the factory to give me the keys. They are a tall, fair-haired, well-dressed couple. He makes his living downtown at the Stock Exchange. Seeing them at the auction, I said a prayer for continued blessings on them. These generous people had allowed us to stay at their luxurious condo until the auction. I knew they must be eager for us to move on, so they could rent the condo for a good income.

My wife sat next to me the entire time, but I could not meet her gaze. I did not want to convey my own shock or disappointment. I whispered to her, "Sit tall, my beloved, and proud. Try to smile."

On my other side, Saba sat on her hands, staring into space. She was in shock, too. I whispered, "Remember, God is watching you now. Try to smile in His light."

"I am trying," she said, not smiling even the slightest. She kept twisting her body around to search the room, as if seeking a friend who never arrived.

Only my innocent son seemed unaffected by the crowd's attention. He sat in his chair, happily reading comic books. Surely he did not understand what this new crime meant for us. This is an example of the purity of children, yes? They live each moment, caring only about the present. Perhaps our hearts become corrupt when we focus too much on the future, on plans and desired outcomes, rather than being grateful for what we have now.

The auction lasted two hours, but the time seemed shorter. A blur of items and bidding and constant knocking of the auctioneer's gavel. Everything sold, even the cast-off junk. By the end, the auction raised approximately fifty thousand dollars. God had provided. Not a fortune, but nearly my annual salary.

I signed the auctioneer's contract again, verifying the sum. Per the contract, we would receive eighty percent, or forty thousand dollars. I wondered how quickly that sum would dwindle and disappear, like a flickering candle on our supper table. Much of it would be *zakat*, a donation for the poor. At the thought of that, my heart began to feel light again.

Afterwards, when the gymnasium emptied, Mr. and Mrs. Musgrove approached us. They had not bid on any items at the auction. This surprised me. They have so much money, and they had gone to the trouble of attending. Mrs. Musgrove wore an elegant pin on the lapel of her coat, a bird made of red and white gems that sparkled under the high gymnasium lights.

I introduced my wife to them, thanked them for coming.

"As our donation," Mr. Musgrove said, "we invite you to stay in the condo for the next full calendar year. You are welcome to stay."

"Rent free, of course," added his lovely, smiling wife. "Just to help you get back on your feet."

We hardly had the words to thank them—what remarkable generosity. And may God increase their kindness.

God has provided. We live modestly, and our needs are small.

[He puts on his eyeglasses and rises from his chair.]

Sir, that is all I can tell you, all I remember. I hope it's helpful. I will ask you to be in touch.

Before you go, I have a question for you: How many weeks are needed before this insurance claim will be paid?

That evening, at a below-street-level jukebox
joint near Michigan Avenue,

DR. REGINA STICKMAN, PRINCIPAL,

slides into a wooden booth across from the Tribune *reporter.*

I apologize for being late. Thanks for meeting me at this out-of-the-way place. Well, out of the way for me. I didn't want to inconvenience *you*. That was the whole point!

What are you drinking?

Oh—wonderful, that's my father's drink. During my childhood, my father was principal of Highsmith. Surely you knew that? For twenty years, he ran the place. He worked his way up from a teaching position. When he got hired, he gave up his parents' name. Strikmann. First casually, then formally. He felt pressured to change it. Well, it was a whole different world, wasn't it?

When I became principal, I was very young. Still in my twenties and feeling like my own school days were yesterday. In my father's time, they called the principal "headmaster," like at an English school. Right from the start, I insisted on being called "principal" rather than "headmistress." To my ears, "headmistress" sounds like some elevated rank of concubine.

Truth be told, I was naïve. I assumed that a leader could be friendly with her staff—could be "part of the gang." But when you're the one who has to make all the hard decisions, that isn't possible. In the end, management personifies all the things workers dislike about their jobs. We become scapegoats for every complaint. Any principal will tell you that. Maybe it's the same at newspapers?

Anyway, I asked you to meet me tonight because I need your help. I find myself in the very unlikely position of having to defend my judgment. My board members have been getting all sorts of *questions* about the auction.

Yes, well, as you can imagine, that day was pure shock—indescribable shock to arrive at school that morning and discover the Darger artwork smoldering in a pile of ash. Because then I was forced to confront what I hoped *could not* be true: This was an inside job. I know for a fact that every door was locked. I turned on the security system myself Friday night when I left the building. Believe me, no student holds a master key, or knows the code for the alarm system. The police must now investigate my faculty like never before.

The worst part was when I noticed Louise Denison, the art appraiser who'd been so generous with her time, standing with the Spoon kids, waiting for the event to begin. She waved hello and said she was in town briefly for the holidays. I smiled, but I felt terribly embarrassed to see her again; so much has happened since we saw her in November that I didn't know what to *begin* to say. Plus, I realized that conveying this most recent development to the Khans personally would demand all the strength I had. As far as I was concerned, everyone else could find out secondhand.

But the ruined artwork isn't even why I need your help. That's not the board's concern. As you know, even without those paintings, the auction raised just over fifty thousand dollars. According to the terms of the contract, the school received ten percent. The day of the event, I was issued a check in the amount of five thousand dollars, give or take, for me to use as I see fit.

My board wants to know why I accepted the check. In their view, it looks bad. One board member called me and she said, "Oh Regina, that's not very much money. Why don't you just let the Khans have that money?" Another one said, "Let's give it back, Regina. Five thousand dollars won't mean much to the school, and it will mean so much more to the Khans."

Here's a lesson you can take with you through life: People become most generous when given the opportunity to spend other people's money.

The Khans walked away with forty thousand dollars. Not a small amount, in my humble opinion.

True, five thousand dollars does seem tiny compared to the annual budget of a big school like ours. However, terms are terms. That money belongs to the school. What kind of precedent would it set if I began giving away money to our students and their families? Where would it end?

Excuse me, which Oriental rug? Back at my office? As it happens, we acquired that carpet last year when a generous donation came from an alum, with the clear requirement that the donation be spent on "campus improvements." So be it. I spent some of it on the carpet, yes, but we also planted the box garden and restored the gorgeous terrazzo border around the cafeteria floor.

People criticize me for spending money on improvements like these. "Superficial things," they say dismissively. It shows how little they know about the importance of beauty in society.

Crime drops when flowers get planted in parks. Did you know that? Statistical fact. Here in Chicago, remember, when Mayor Daley made beautification a priority, the crime rate finally began to drop. And by adding more trees and repairing the park fountains and spending a fortune on those foot-high, decorative iron fences everwhere, the city kept getting safer. That's a fact.

The same is true in schools. Trust me, when we simply improve the looks of things, it reduces discipline issues and leads to a sense of pride. You don't have to be an educator to know that personal pride leads to personal success.

So you see, we can change lives—and improve the world—one beautiful carpet at a time.

Besides, I have plans for the five thousand dollars. I'll tell you my secret. There's a neglected grotto in the garden, adjacent to the Shack—crap, I owe myself a quarter—adjacent to *Tarlan's Track*, which would be perfect for a wedding ceremony. I have been dreaming about having an outdoor wedding venue on the property for years. Our campus is ideally located, an oasis of green near the congested downtown. Think of the revenue! Weddings every weekend in the summer, one blushing bride after the next. Receptions on the lawn under elegant tents. Tables and chairs, also available for rent.

After one summer, the venue will pay for itself. The rest will be money in the bank for the school.

No, not for an art collection. Let's start with a new roof!

My point is, I have the *vision*. That's what makes me a leader. I'm looking ahead and I plan to stick around for a long while. Board members, incidentally, are the ones who come and go. They only last about four years, same as the students.

Anyway, what I'd really like is for you to write something about my new project. After the holidays, of course. Obviously we don't want to leave this story as it is, sitting like a horrible pile of ashes on the floor of my gymnasium. The senseless destruction of artwork is not the story. How could it be? The story is the *beauty* that may appear as a result. Beauty and ongoing value to the school. That's the far more important takeaway here, wouldn't you say?

Ready for another drink?

To art!

*Meanwhile, in a musty-smelling basement
rec room across town,*

STEVE DAVINSKI, SENIOR,

*plays pool with his brother Don, age 11,
and tells it like it is.*

For me, Dawg, the hardest thing in the world is letting a girl down when things aren't working out.

It goes against my nature to make girls sad. I'm the guy who makes things better, right? It's like I've got this list of job duties at school: "game winner," "problem solver," "leader," "hero." And sometimes, unfortunately, that list includes "heartbreaker."

This girl and I only went out for a couple of months. Kept things real friendly, to say the least. We had some fun together, and it was super cool to be around someone like Saba. Different from the girls I normally date. Exotic. She has this weird combination of innocence and spice. Sort of like sweet-and-sour chicken, you know? Totally awesome, but . . . whatever.

When the auction came, I needed to pull the plug. The timing was wrong. Really, all along that was the problem: timing. Saba had her whole "family drama" thing going on, and I had basketball and student government and my college applications to finish. We both got busy. It happens, right?

College applications, I mean, that's what put me over the edge. Since October, I've been getting major heat from Mom and Dad, the college counselors, my coaches—just about everyone, really—to get those suckers turned in early. But every time I sit down to write the application essays, my brain freezes. I can't think what to write. It's like I don't have any relevant stories to tell. All I know about is playing sports and being popular, and those things don't count for squat when it comes to getting into college.

So today I stopped Saba in the hall between periods. I told her that things were looking really busy over the holidays, and I was *super* bummed, but I wouldn't be able to hang out again, just the two of us, for a while. I promised her we'd stay friends—which is basically all we ever were, okay?

She didn't say a word. She just looked at me as if I'd puked on her shoes or something.

Don't get me wrong. Like I said, I know the timing is bad. No question, she's had a rough year. First the theft, and the auction, and now this? But from my experience with girls, I've learned it's best to end things as fast as possible. Like ripping off a Band-Aid. The way I see it, I'm doing her a favor. If she can't see that now, she will later, when she thinks back on the killer times we had together. I was a stand-up guy, and she'll remember that.

I do feel guilty. Dawg, I feel like crap. But the thing is, I'm at a place where I need to focus on my future, the way everybody tells me. Now's the time to put *me first* for once. Time to seize the opportunities I've made for myself. Give me some credit—I've worked like hell for four years. When the game begins, you have to stop talking to the cheerleaders and get your ass onto the court. That's how the game gets played, am I right?

The following day, FRIDAY, DECEMBER 21,
a half-day before the winter break,

SABA KHAN, SOPHOMORE,

texts the following five messages
to Steve Davinski, senior.

7:58 a.m.
So hey . . . yesterday u surprised me. I was 2
shocked 2 respond. We can figure this out! Let's
talk.

11:32 a.m.
WTF? I can't believe u just turned + walked
the other way when you saw me! Is that how a
man acts? Txt so we can talk! U owe me that, at
least.

3:51 p.m.
OK ur busy. I get this is crunch time. Maybe we
can chill over break + talk? I really need to see
u. I will even bring breakfast? ☺

7:10 p.m.
Seriously, what is up? Why don't u txt back?
This is SO stupid. I feel awful.

10:22 p.m.
This is just to say, I hear u loud and clear. The silence tells me all I need to know abt us and abt u. + that is helpful. Hope u get everything u deserve.

Hard lessons on Highsmith curriculum

YOU'VE heard me brag about the basketball team at the Highsmith School, my alma mater, for more years than we need to calculate, thank you very much. But no sports talk today, folks.

The school is closed now for winter break. If I took you to visit the picturesque campus today, we'd see only winding footpaths covered in snow, the lagoon frozen over with ice, and the doors of the grand old buildings locked for a well-deserved rest.

Students at Highsmith learned a painfully cold lesson this month: Even when a community works together with good intentions toward a worthy goal, opposition may be encountered.

As multiple sources have reported, Highsmith students hosted a benefit on December 15 in support of a classmate whose home was lost in a fire. Just before the event, after weeks of planning and promoting, the most valuable auction item—a booklet of drawings by legendary Chicago "outsider artist" Henry Darger—was stolen and destroyed.

"Pure shock—indescribable shock." This was how the school's principal, Dr. Regina Stickman, expressed her reaction upon learning the artwork had been destroyed. Even now, no arrests have been made. In fact, neither school authorities nor police investigators have identified any clear motive for the crime.

My take on it? A December prank this cold-hearted can only be credited to a different kind of outsider: a Grinch.

As most readers know, Dr. Seuss's beloved 1957 children's book relates the tale of a miserable old hermit who tries to "steal Christmas" from a neighboring town.

The Grinch fails, of course. In the wake of his looting, the people of the town still sing, still celebrate, still believe. Certain things cannot be stolen.

Fortunately, Highsmith's holiday tale also has an uplifting ending.

Despite the crime, the school benefit managed to raise approximately $50,000—a sum that will provide significant comfort to this family in crisis. According to Dr. Stickman, a small portion of the money has even been earmarked for campus improvements. Now that's a heartwarming story, no matter how you read it.

If we could visit Highsmith today, I would lead you down the silent corridors until we came to a striking seal on the floor, a blood-red H carved in stone. This hallowed seal represents the sacred Honor of every student who spends four years at Highsmith.

The stone seal is indelible, consecrated by the generations of alumnae who have passed by, understanding and believing. No outsider, no matter how cunning, can ever steal that belief away.

Bob Bishop, columnist, *Chicago Tribune*, December 23

On *DECEMBER 25, in a yellow farmhouse kitchen*
where an obscenely large turkey is roasting,

JAVIER CONEJERA, SOPHOMORE,

uses an ancient desktop computer to
write to his friend Jennifer.

Now we are in Wisconsin, at the house of my host
grandmother. My brothers and I sleep in camping
sacks in the basement. We will be five days here.

My host grandmother, Nancy, is very tall, of course,
like her children, like the pine trees outside. She is
the first American I met who smokes! Last evening,
when we arrived, I went outdoors to smoke, and
she followed me with her own cigarettes. We did not
talk together. I think she is shy like me. Instead we
stood and looked at the snow covering the trees and
fields with white. There are no neighbors on neither
side of this house, only nature. I feel far away from
Chicago here. I will enjoy this place for a while,
surrounded by trees and birds, and some occasions
for quietness.

This morning, while the others moved to separate corners to play with their new games and to wash new clothes, I called my mother. For her I described Nancy's belén, which is on the floor in the living room—not just a barn with animals and Los Reyes Magos, but a complete village of ceramics, with houses, bank, church, school, ice cream shop, train and tracks, and the Jesus baby in His barn in the middle—a size bigger than all the other items, because He is made from a different company.

Mama asked if Papa Noel had come, and I told her yes, he brought a package of chocolates and money all the way from España! She pretended the surprise. I did not want to tell her that this money will pay for library books that fools damaged in snow for no reason. It was good to hear Mama's voice.

And now, Jen, the most incredible part: If I tell you that Steve has been transformed by the holiday spirit, will you believe me?

This morning, when we awoke in our camping sacks, he sat up, rubbed the eyes, and said, "Oh, hey bro, Feliz Navidad." Later at Mass, he embraced me and wished me peace. And most surprising of all, when we came back to Nancy's house, Steve gave me a card. The note says: "Javier, I realize the past few months have been difficult for you. I am sorry for not being the perfect host brother. But I believe in second chances, and I will try to make things better when we get back to school, especially after the basketball season is over in February. Merry Christmas." I believe we can call this a miracle of Christmas, no?

Steve promises to make things better for me when we return to school, but I fear it is too late. Is a "second chance" possible? Jen, I want to tell you something now. I must confess what I have done or be miserable. I wanted to tell Mama, but I do not have the courage to say something that will give her pain.

Here is what happened: For many days, I felt anger when I was at the school. Anger, because of the library books. Anger, because of the absurd accusations. Anger, because I have failed to discover the life here that America advertises to people all over the world—a life of friends and community and hope. Instead, at the school I observe only fire, theft, destruction, and the faces that always turn away from me.

Moreover, near my locker, that seal on the floor! How this seal tormented me, the students giving me the rude, forceful bumps in order to avoid the sacred H. My anger grew like a disease inside the body. These students are hypocrites, I think. They are lying hypocrites without worth.

On the last Friday before the holiday, the school was empty by noon. I always avoid the crowded bus, a bus of cold eyes and sharp elbows, and usually I wait for some time before I go outside. On that day, the hallway had cleared, but I stood by my locker and stared at the hypocritical seal, thinking how this letter on the floor had become my enemy.

Without warning, I did something risky and stupid. I hardly believe I did it. My actions were not "premeditated," like the crimes on the TV shows favored by the Davinskis. I did not think with reason.

One can of aerosol paint from the auction remained in my locker. Taking the paint, I stepped to the center of the hallway. I looked around and saw no one. Careful not to step on the H, of course, (that would be rude) I bent down and covered the H with the white paint. I made big circles, over and over—soft round white curls, like a ghost, the ghost of something dead. Maybe Kendra is correct. Maybe I am an artist after all.

I know, Jen—this action lacked purpose, like throwing water into the sea. And the administrators will catch me for certain. Like a fool, I put the aerosol can back into my locker. When I return to Highsmith, the students finally will despise me for a reason that is legitimate. Now I never will be part of that community. The difference is, now it is a situation I choose for myself, not by other people. Will that make it easier? I think yes.

Nancy is going outside to smoke. I will join her—I must enjoy the peace while it lasts. This is the most strange Christmas. I hope yours is normal.

JEAN DELACROIX,
DEPARTMENT OF ART,

Lord have mercy. More questions about this? You are as bad as Ms. Ames.

Well, to give Ms. Ames credit, her statement proved to have some value.

Detective, you've shown them my own statement by now? Yes, I've openly admitted it: The person who removed the paintings from the gym office was me. I moved the album to the art annex without telling anyone. In retrospect, this was poor judgment, I see that now. But it was a spontaneous instinct—to protect it.

You felt justified taking it without permission?

I did! We were keeping an *art treasure* in the gym office, even after I pointed out its value. After word got out about the paintings, the school was crawling with journalists, collectors,

Darger devotees. And still, we decided to leave these paintings unprotected in the gym? I felt some individual responsibility to help keep the album safe. After all, I was the one who discovered it.

Jean, why didn't you talk to me about your concerns?

Dr. Stickman, I did speak to you. More than once. With all due respect, you brushed me off like I was griping about the broken kiln again. I figured it was easier to move the album without permission and then ask for forgiveness later. The fact that I had no problem walking out of the gym with it shows that *anybody* could have done the same thing.

But nobody else did. You did. And between the time you took it and the time it was returned, it was destroyed.

I can't explain that. All I know is—okay, yes, Ariel surely did hold the artwork in her hands, between the folds of a quilt, on the Friday afternoon when she came to ask for a ride. My plan was to take it home that night for safekeeping until the auction. But considering the snow, it didn't seem smart to take it outdoors and risk getting it wet. So I left it here and gave Ariel her ride.

And you waited until Monday to come back for it?

No, obviously I came back to school first thing on Saturday to get it, but by then the album had disappeared from my room.

It was gone! I searched everywhere, frantic, but couldn't find it. And I couldn't *say* anything without looking responsible for losing it. I assumed it would turn up, that whoever had taken it from me would be caught right away. But the school reported it stolen so quickly—

"Stolen" seems like the appropriate word for what happened.

Maybe it seems so, but I'm asking you to consider *intention*. My plan was never to keep the album or sell it, only to protect it until it could be sold. Detective, when your men confiscated my own work, I panicked. I came clean and told you everything. But you didn't believe me. You seemed convinced I had stashed it someplace to sell at a later date. I gave you my keys so you could search my apartment and my car, but of course we never found it.

Well—not until it was returned.

Talk to the detective. Multiple sources will corroborate my story: I was nowhere near school the weekend of the auction. I may have made one bad decision, but trust me, I'm going to be cleared of any wrongdoing. How have I profited from any of this? I still haven't gotten my own work back! Granted, since I lied initially about my involvement, I understand why I'm getting these questions. But there's absolutely nothing more I can tell you.

Sir, we're just trying to understand what happened to the artwork.

I would love to know! I'm sick about it. Ask twenty members of the faculty, and you'll get twenty different answers about what's happened here and why. The only valuable thing this experience has helped me to understand is Darger's own work. Some art scholars maintain that it is impossible to fully appreciate a piece of art unless you consider the artist's childhood.

Childhood? We're not talking about anyone's childhood. We're talking about a serious crime.

In Darger's case, what's the difference? Just hear me out for a second, folks. Darger was born in Chicago in 1892, the son of a disabled tailor. When Henry was a toddler, his mother died, and his father put Henry's only sibling, a *baby sister*, up for adoption. Henry never saw the girl again. What do you make of that—a boy loses his baby sister and spends the rest of his life endlessly drawing pictures of these strong, heroic, beautiful little girls?

Frankly it seems a little weird to me. Then again, I'm not an artist.

When Henry was eight, his father became too ill to care for him. He sent Henry to a Catholic home for orphaned boys, but the nuns threw him out for fighting and odd behavior. Here's where the story gets really dark: Against his will, Henry was moved to Lincoln, Illinois, several hours from

Chicago, to an asylum for "feeble-minded" children. This was no school—it was a grueling work farm, where thousands of kids labored all day, under threats of violence.

Sounds terrible, Jean. Gentlemen, I think we are finished here . . .

Not long after Henry arrived, he got word that his father died. This left Henry an orphan, completely alone in the world—alone *except* for the long-lost baby sister. Or, the notion of her. The very possibility of her survival must have fed Henry's private daydreams. As long as her adventure story continued, Henry would never be totally alone. Henry remained at that asylum for seven long years. He was fifteen before he could make his escape and return to Chicago. At seventeen, he found work at a hospital—janitor, dishwasher—menial jobs he kept for nearly six decades, until he was too old to work.

And speaking of work, gentlemen . . .

How can our hearts not be touched by this picture of a sensitive kid like Henry Darger, locked up in a horrendous children's asylum? Can any of us understand the isolation, the helplessness that kid must have felt? Sometimes, when you lose your freedom, that's when your fiercest dreams are born—dreams that can feed your imagination for the rest of your life.

A fascinating art history lesson, Jean, but I'm sure everyone's time is valuable. We need to be clear: You're absolutely sure that the artwork was hidden in the annex when you left school that Friday?

Positive. And by the time I returned the next morning, it was gone. I'll swear to it under oath. I'll take a polygraph test, or do whatever it takes to prove *once and for all* that I am telling the truth. Otherwise, I'm done answering your questions. Listen, my time is valuable, too. Ever since I discovered those Darger paintings, I've been in constant contact with art experts around the country. I've got a story to tell—a story people want to hear. I've had speaking and writing invitations that will allow me to give up teaching altogether, so I can spend more time creating my own pieces.

The quilts, you mean, sir.

My fiber art projects, yes. I was going to submit them for a show in Paris. It's too late for that now, of course. All I know, Dr. Stickman, is that I'll be leaving Highsmith at the end of the year. You'll be getting my official letter of resignation soon.

A bit later, at separate tables in the faculty lunchroom,

WENDY PINCH & ARIEL AMES

lead similar conversations in different directions.

WENDY:

Naturally I wasn't thrilled to hear my aunt had dropped dead, but I'm grateful for the opportunity she left me. I'm retiring at the end of the year. And that means no more grading, no more going over basic game rules with little turds who never want to move a muscle. No more driving the unreliable school vans to basketball tournaments in snowstorms.

ARIEL:

The week after the auction, the only laugh I had was when I read an essay from one of my students on *The Great Gatsby*. Kendra Spoon did a creative comparison of Jay Gatsby and Harold from *Harold and the Purple Crayon*—her two "favorite" visionary dreamers. She made connections between Harold's pies and Gatsby's lovely shirts, between Harold's apples that will never turn red, because they're drawn in purple, and the unreachable green light at the end of Daisy's dock. Brilliant! Seriously, love that girl.

WENDY:

Only problem is, I hate to leave under what only can be described as a dark cloud. People are still looking at me funny, even though I didn't profit from this Harvey Dooley business in any way. All I got was a stain on the gym floor where that guy's mess got dumped. My souvenir, I guess.

ARIEL:

I'm furious about what happened. Kendra and her brother worked so hard to organize that event. We all pitched in. For the first time, I felt proud to be part of the Highsmith team. And while the universe seemed to reward this effort by giving us a big-ticket item like the Darger album, someone else decided to intervene and ruin everything. It all seems so mean, so personal.

WENDY:

Tell you the truth, my heart broke a little bit when I saw the kids at the auction—Saba Khan coming with her family, the Spoon kids standing with their proud mama—and knowing how this cuckoo crime would affect all of them.

ARIEL:

The weirdest part was the quiet, didn't you think? The week after the auction? The kids were in shock. It was like the entire community had suffered this punch in the stomach. Before break, some kid even *spray-painted* the school seal in the central corridor! I mean, that isn't normal behavior.

WENDY:

My gut tells me this was motivated by race. This was a hate crime, see? It's the only way I can figure it. Someone hated the thought of the Khans getting rich *just because some jackass torched their apartment. It didn't seem fair that these relative newcomers could be so lucky. Why else would a person steal the art, rip it to shreds, then burn it? That kind of anger is a little scary, don't you think?*

ARIEL:

The poor Spoons! Someone resented those kids so much, they didn't want to see this auction succeed. I've seen it happen before. When someone does something particularly well, or thinks outside the box, or goes the extra mile, it can make other people feel bad about themselves. It's true.

WENDY:

I'm not talking about ordinary jealousy. We pretend to be this diverse nation of tolerance, the great Melting Pot. But deep down, a lot of people mistrust a neighbor who doesn't "fit in" or look the same. It's not a melting pot so much as a scummy hotel Jacuzzi, where no one wants to get too close to the other guy, because who knows where the heck he's been? You know what I'm saying.

ARIEL:

Can I be honest? When I first got here, I was so excited. My brain was spinning with ideas, like a tornado. But every time I made a suggestion at an English team meeting, I got shot down. Over and over, they said, "We can't do that." Or, "That won't work here." Big discovery: Nobody likes it when someone *new* offers fresh ideas for improving the system. That's what happened to the Spoons. The "new kids" had the idea, so *the idea could not succeed.* It might have been different if it was a legacy family that led the effort—the grandson or granddaughter of one of those grim, dumb faces hanging on the wall in the main lobby.

WENDY:

You think Saba Khan has it easy here at Highsmith? She's this friendly, good-looking, intelligent girl. A real ace on the tennis court, too. Saba makes an honest effort to connect with people. But when I see her—standing at her locker, or moving through the cafeteria line—usually she's alone. She comes alive at tennis matches, but I never see the girl at extracurricular events. Not at dances or basketball games, nothing.

ARIEL:

By any standard, what the Spoons accomplished is incredible. They helped to draw our attention to a family tragedy right in our community. They united the whole school and got the attention of the press. They brought out the best in all of us. And it all started in *my* classroom.

WENDY:

I'll give you that. Saba may stay home by her own choice. But imagine it from her view. Saba's been in this country her whole life, but is she included? *Every day at school, by their distance and their polite silences, her peers tell her: Welcome to America, honey. You may never truly fit in here. I heard a rumor last month that Saba was hanging out with Steve Davinski. Impossible! First, Saba is traditional. Her parents are on the job, see? No way is Saba stepping out with a boy. But second, a couple like Saba and Steve Davinski could never exist at Highsmith. The division lines separating the social groups are darn near impossible to cross.*

ARIEL:

Jean Delacroix. Yeah, that was unfortunate. And sure, I have regrets about it. I wish things had gone differently. I made a point to go and apologize. It was important to me to clear the air . . . Not right away, no. My schedule was crazy, and I was swamped with essays to read. Plus, Jean and

I have different lunch schedules, and we never see each other ordinarily. In retrospect, I did commit a bit of a faux pas by waiting until there was another snowstorm, a real terror of a blizzard. I realized it would take me forever to get home on the bus when there was heavy, drifting snow like that.

That same day, during his study hall—
his last study hall—

JAVIER CONEJERA, SOPHOMORE,

writes to his friend Jennifer in Oklahoma.
He deliberately uses the computer workstation reserved
for catalog searches.

Hola Jen,

For two weeks, I waited with dread for this day
to arrive. Every day, I think my host parents will
receive the angry telephone call from the principal,
informing them of my foolish crime. Informing them
of my punishment. This telephone call never came.
Maybe the principal was on a holiday too.

Moreover, this morning before school, I went to my
locker and discovered a surprise: The sacred seal
is clean again! The floor surrounding the H shines
under the hallway lights. There is no evidence of
my mistake. For several seconds, I wondered if my
action was only a wishful fantasy, a vivid daydream.

Then I opened my locker. The can of white aerosol paint was not where I put it. At the same time, a loud announcement in the hallway ordered me to the office of the principal.

I did not walk slowly. I felt no anxiety. At last, I was ready.

The principal met me in the reception area and led me back into her office. As soon as I sat in a big chair, I observed on her desk the aerosol paint. Of course.

The principal said, "Javier, during the break, we found this paint in your locker. I must ask you, did you put the paint on the floor?"

I said yes. Well, I am not a liar.

She looked at me, as if waiting for me to say more. I had nothing more to say. The principal leaned the body forward in the chair: "And why did you do this?"

The truth, Jen, I do not have the words to explain. How do I express the emotions that inspired me to do something so foolish? My action was not rational. It was personal. All I know, on that day I felt the anger. I felt the frustration. I felt no hope in this place.

The principal continued, "Javier, you covered up the school seal. This symbol is respected by every student in this school. We were required to hire professionals to come and clean the floor. This costs money. Do you have anything to say?" (No.) "Nothing?" I looked at her. Nothing. I had nothing to tell her, nothing she will understand.

Jen, do you remember in my village, the church tower? The bell rings for various reasons. Many tourists who visit the village hear the bell and believe it is marking a new hour, or calling them to Mass. But the locals know the padre sometimes rings the bell for no reason. The old man is completely senile. Sometimes a bell rings because a man wants to ring the bell.

The principal sat waiting for an answer, the same as the entire community of Highsmith waits, all the people waiting for the same thing. For answers that may never come.

She said, "Very well. This is a serious offense, which merits a severe punishment. You will have a detention every day after school between now and spring break. On Saturdays, you will work with our custodians to clean the building."

There is a big calendar on her desk, the same as the calendar in the kitchen of my host family. I watch as the principal writes my name, over and over, on all the Saturdays. She wants me to see this—to make sure I understand what I have done and what I will do.

Of course, I prepared for this moment. I expected this. From my pocket, I take the money that I had been saving to come see you. $300. I put it on the desk, in the middle of the calendar. "To help pay for the extra cleaning," I say. This is the only thing I say. I do not argue about the detentions or the Saturdays with the custodians, because—well, why? I get up and leave her office without giving another word.

After, on the door of my locker, I find a face drawn with a black Sharpie—a face with eyes that are angry—the glare of a student who knows I put the paint on the sacred H. Or one who still believes I destroyed the paintings by Henry Darger. Or both. For many weeks, this crime prevented me from finding my place here. And now I am responsible too.

Jen, this is the last email I will send from Chicago. Tonight I will fill my suitcases again. On Wednesday I will go back to O'Hare Airport so that I may return to my country before the school term begins there. When I called my mother to tell her, she argued with me. She did not want to change the ticket, because of the expense. She said it is normal to be homesick. Then she heard the tears in my voice and she understood. She said, "Come home."

One feels sadness when a dream dies, and also relief.

Today is the day for quitting. At lunch, I saw my friend Kendra sitting at a table with her many friends. Although Kendra has been a student at Highsmith for the same time as me, she is accepted now, even popular. I waited for friendships to come to me, but she did not wait. She worked with strength and made intelligent choices to reach this goal.

I wanted to say good-bye. We stepped away from the table so we could talk in private. I told her my plan to go, and she nodded without speaking, not with surprise, not with disappointment, as if she understood.

I told her I would not be able to provide the tutoring in Spanish as I promised before the auction. "Don't worry," she said. She frowned and rubbed the forehead, as if embarrassed. "The weird thing was, no one bid on it."

"No one?" I said, and then smiled very fast to show this news does not hurt my feelings. Not too much.

"So I bid on it!" she said, her voice cheerful again. "I mean, I was excited to buy it. I need the help."

"I am very sorry, then," I said, and this was true. "At least, I can promise to give you the tutoring when you come to visit me in España someday."

"Definitely," she said, as she hugged me good-bye.

Kendra and I never went to the tapas café, even though she said we would do that, too. "Definitely." Maybe we would have gone if I remained in Chicago for a full second term. It was friendly to say we would go.

On Saturday, when I informed my host family that I will be returning to España so soon, they pretended the disappointment. Mrs. Davinski said, "But, Savior, you're going to miss so much. Baseball season hasn't even started. Wrigley Field!"

I will miss some things. I will miss the adventure of living in a strange city. I will miss the pride I found in surviving each day, the satisfaction of getting from one place to another place without getting lost, and the exhilaration of using a foreign language to communicate. I will miss Kendra, who always offered to help, and quiet Nancy who shared her cigarettes and never judged me. I will even miss my host family. They have given me a lifetime of excellent stories to tell. So then, no regrets.

Except one! Amiga, I am not able to visit you over the Spring Break now. This disappoints me too. But I know you understand. And I will make it there someday—definitely.

With love from your friend, who is going home at last.

SABA KHAN, SOPHOMORE,

*adds what she can to her own written chronicle of
these turns of events.*

This high-rise still doesn't feel like home. The whole year can pass by + this temporary condo will always feel foreign to me: sleeping in someone else's bed, brushing my teeth in front of some other girl's mirror.

I seek out signs that things will be normal again: My hair finally has grown back to the length it was before the Fenwick match. The weird, pitying hellos from strangers have dwindled off. + today at lunch, when I offered to treat for nachos, the girls sat back with their arms folded + they <u>let</u> me pay. "Extra peppers!" Beti called. I wanted to hug her.

For a few weeks after the auction, my family adopted a strategy: Do nothing. "For now, babies, we put this drama out of our minds," Ammi said. At her urging, we began playing games again, the ordinary kind with cards + dice, the ones that clearly determine a winner. The check from the auctioneer sat on the dining room table until after New Year's, tucked in a silver napkin holder that came with this place. At some point, the check disappeared — deposited into the bank account, more money than the account has ever seen.

This past weekend, Ammi filled the teakettle + fried some bread with brown sugar. With these treats, she lured us all into the living room, where we piled onto the sofa, a family pile — even Salman, who usually is too hyper to relax. He picked up the remote control + pointed it at the TV. Suddenly the gas logs in the fireplace burst with flickering orange flames.

"Hey, we have already seen this program!" Papa said. This has become a dependable joke. "OK, let us talk about the future."

We cuddled on the sofa, watching the fire + we made a plan. "Only a dummy quits a good job," Papa said. Of course he'll keep working at the factory. The money from the auction will remain in the bank, minus a contribution for the poor.

At the end of this year, we'll use the auction money as a down payment on a condo. Nothing too big. Nothing with marble in the bathrooms or million-dollar views. Nothing we can't afford. We want to be back in the old neighborhood — closer to the Pakistani shops + our mosque.

I asked, "If there's any left, can we at least get . . . a new car?"

Papa said, "Do not think about what might be, or what might have been. Yes, we might have been rich—so what? It's done."

"We might still be rich," I said under my breath, thinking about insurance money.

Papa's voice was gentle but persuasive: "Time to forget about that. We are rich in a different way. + besides, those questions will drive us mad. Only God knows why someone took the art + destroyed it. Only God knows why the school administration did not keep it somewhere safe."

I wanted to say, No—not only God knows. Someone else knows these things. That's what makes the situation so infuriating.

We are victims here. Why isn't he angry about that? Me, I'm getting used to the role. 1 week I'm hanging out with the most popular boy in school, feeling like Cinderella at the ball + the next week, old Prince Charmless turns back into an ordinary giant. Drops me without any reason, except that he's . . . "too busy"? His attitude took me by such extreme surprise that I literally didn't know what to say or how to feel. It's been 3 weeks + I still don't. It was beyond messed up. Now I wonder if "the creeping vine" + I ever had anything real at all . . .

My girls tell me to take it in stride. Kendra especially. She says: "You're Steve Davinski's ex. Saba stock is through the roof!"

Maybe that's true. I appreciate Kendra for trying to make me smile. But it doesn't change the way my heart feels.

Today I left an obscenely huge chocolate bar in Kendra's locker. My note said, "Here's a big sweet reward for being you!"

She'll never suspect, but it was an apology. For too long, I was annoyed at Kendra + her brother. I actually felt angry that they were _helping_. That wasn't fair. Without the Spoons, my family might be living in a shelter right now. True, helping might have come easily for them, but the Spoons made everything happen for us. Almost as if they understood how hard it is to come to your own aid. How overwhelming it feels when everything goes wrong. It can paralyze a person!

The funny thing is, Kendra + I are total opposites. I'm an introvert, she can talk to anyone. We come from completely different backgrounds. Still, we have this weird bond. Kendra seemed to see it first. From the very beginning of the tennis season, she latched on to me, even off the court. Since she was new, I figured she only needed a friend, any friend. But then, after the fire, Kendra was the 1st person who stepped up to say she would help. The girl changed my life.

Despite all that's happened, I feel hopeful. Because when the Spoons get a check from the insurance company, they will give us that money. They were willing to donate the art, so why wouldn't they donate the money?

$500,000. All those zeroes, like tiny windows into our

future. I peer into them and see: Now we will stay in this tricked-out condo with this huge bedroom + the view of the park + tennis courts + it will be ours. We'll get a new car, with smooth leather seats + dependable heat. College costs, completely paid for, for both Salman + me. We'll take a trip to Pakistan to meet family I've only heard about in stories, like characters in a book.

+ when we step off the airplane in Islamabad + the cousins surround us, they will know right away, by the way we dress + our heavy bags filled with expensive gifts, that we truly are an American success story.

On the evening of TUESDAY, JANUARY 15,
at a rented townhouse filled with boxes,

KEVIN SPOON, SENIOR,

opens the door and finds the insurance investigator,
who carries a file of papers.

Oh hey. My mom's still at work, but she'll be home in . . . twenty minutes? If you want to stick around so you can go over those papers with her, that's cool with me. I know she's been waiting for them.

Yeah, sit anywhere. Move that stuff to make space, if you need to.

Tell you the truth, I was never sure what exactly insurance *was* until we had to buy some. I guess you guys come in after the fact and save the day, huh? That's got to be an excellent feeling.

Isn't it weird how people are *defined* by the way they make money? By their jobs? Put it this way: My mom works in sales, and that's who she is. You work in insurance, and that's who you are. My teachers work in education, and it might as well be written on their tombstones someday. Like, "Here Lies Edith Jones, Beloved AP Human Geography Teacher." They should do that, right? It would make cemeteries more interesting. "Here Lies Benjamin Smith, Gifted Orthodontist." "R.I.P. Bill Green, Who Sold Toyotas Throughout the Greater Chicagoland Area."

My sister Kendra wants to be a baby photographer. She's obsessed with babies. She wants to have a cool loft studio filled with fancy equipment and enough toys to keep all the hipster babies giggling. *Or* she wants to be a nurse on a cancer ward. I can just picture her, awake in the middle of the night, fighting back tears as she valiantly rubs Lubriderm onto the foot of a sleeping patient.

When she was little, she wanted to be the person whose job it was to polish the crown jewels for some rich European nation. She saw herself wearing a little black apron, buffing up the crowns, scepters and rings, and reporting: "Your Majesty, the jewels are sparkling and ready for wear."

My sister's full of ideas—but me? No clue. Obviously, based on this past winter, I do not suck at fundraising. I could work for a charity.

Unlike Kendra, when I try to picture my life after college, all I see is a blank screen. My mom says, "You start by collecting your props." She tells me to picture my hands: What will I be holding in my hands someday?

Maybe a paintbrush. Those are my art supplies over there. I'd take over the whole house if Mom let me. No matter where we've lived, I've always painted. I do think about making art in the future, but not so much about how I'll pay bills. Kendra tells me I need to think practically—that I need a plan—which is annoying. She's like my mom. She could always sell air.

Speaking of which, yeah, pardon all the boxes everywhere. Actually my mom got another job offer. Atlanta. I guess Atlanta rush-hour traffic is awful, which means long commutes, which means more time in cars, which means more expensive radio advertising. So now we'll be moving again.

Honestly, it's frustrating. Especially for Kendra. We killed ourselves last fall to become part of this community, working like crazy to make friends and to stand out in a positive way—and all for what? For Atlanta? Please.

Yeah, we helped the Khans. That counts for something. As Kendra said, no one else was going to take a *magic purple crayon* and draw a better life for Saba Khan, or for anyone. So we drew it. Someone had to, right?

I'm telling you, if you've earned people's trust and work as a team, there's nothing you can't accomplish.

That's why it's super annoying to have to start all over again. It's not a good feeling, you know, when nothing's in your control.

Did you ever look at those Darger paintings? It was easy for us to relate to those kids, the ones fighting against the grown-ups, the same ones who always run everything. The grown-ups who want to determine our future for us.

I don't mean to complain. Generally, when I think about the future, I feel hopeful. My mom says it's not enough to hope. She says we need to plan—and take risks and make sacrifices and be ruthless. Or else, what? Watch our personal goals fade over time until there's nothing left but a *memory* of the goal? An old "what if?" That would suck.

Anyway, yeah, Saba Khan's doing fine now. I mean, better than fine. We made sure her situation turned out okay. That was important.

And now, I don't know . . . this insurance thing . . .

Let's not forget, Saba's had advantages we haven't had. For one thing, she's lived in the same city her whole life. I really envy that. My family never stops moving, and Saba has a home. She has a community. And she has a dad! But we've done okay. My mom makes up for it. I'm not complaining. Put it this way: Everybody gets a different mix, right? We made sure Saba—

Oh, wait. Sorry. Here's my mom now. . . .

Nice talking to you, sir.

*On FRIDAY, JANUARY 25, after bouncing
a basketball for twenty minutes for no good reason
in the gym lobby,*

STEVE DAVINSKI, SENIOR,

*takes a seat on a bench next to an unfamiliar man who
turns out to be the insurance investigator.*

Aw, no way! So, if I understand the facts correctly, you're stuck with a mystery on your hands. A gigantic, expensive, embarrassing mystery.

No disrespect, sir, but I'm betting the big boss at the office doesn't cheer for a loss. Am I right?

In my life, I don't play much with odds or speculation. Me, I only shoot when I'm confident I can make the basket. I solve equations using the facts I know.

But this mess we've had at school this year . . . It hasn't always been easy to keep score, you know? Nothing's been clear.

Like, see this ball here? Well, actually, you don't. You only see *one side* of the ball. The only way you ever see the whole thing is like this.

[Spins the basketball on his finger.]

That's Coach P's favorite trick. Before each game, she stands in the locker room and spins the ball on her finger. She says, "Players, here's what you gotta think about if you want to win today." She tells us if we work as a team and watch the ball from every side, we're golden.

Suppose I was playing your little guessing game—*Who Screwed Everything Up?* One thing we know now, for example, is that we can rule out my old roommate. A grand *adios* to Javier. Guess I was wrong about him. Yeah, the kid had sticky fingers, thanks to the spray paint, but he wasn't a thief. He was a loner, but harmless enough. He walked away empty-handed.

My guess? Like everything else, it all comes down to numbers. Cold hard cash. According to my dad, money motivates Americans. It's what brings people to this country. Face it, nobody ever comes to the good ole U. S. of A. in search of spiritual enlightenment.

The Khans came here to make money and to give their kids access to the best education in the world. Will they get it here at Highsmith? Depends who you ask. But if Saba takes the opportunity and gets the best education she can, I guarantee Saba will make her money down the road. And so will I. Look at me, I'm playing the game.

So follow the money.

Don't look at me—I got squat.

Yeah, Saba's family got their forty grand, and can live in a swank apartment for a year, rent-free. Happy ending for them.

And Principal Stickman got herself some cash to build a tacky little wedding chapel outside.

Our coach is retiring early, thanks to some inheritance money. And Mr. Delacroix, the art teacher—he's giving up teaching and plans to pursue his own dreams.

But in the big picture? That's all peanuts.

After all is said and done, who came out ahead? Who made the money?

DR. REGINA STICKMAN, PRINCIPAL,

dated MONDAY, JANUARY 28.

To United Insurance:

Sorry I missed your call. I wish I could help you. As of last Friday, January 25, the Spoons are no longer enrolled at Highsmith. At present, we have no forwarding information for the family. If that changes, I certainly will be in touch.

To the *Chicago Tribune*:

Sorry I missed you! To answer your question, I can confirm that the Spoons are no longer enrolled here. Mrs. Spoon came in on Friday. Apparently she asked for their first semester transcripts, then pulled the kids out of class. That's all I know. To be honest, I'm ready to draw the curtain closed on that little drama. This time of year, we at Highsmith are looking ahead, not behind. Our seniors are getting into excellent, selective colleges and we celebrate good news as it arrives.

I'm genuinely sorry I missed your call, because I am eager to chat again. Do you want to put together a story about the wedding venue planned for our campus? I've met with a contractor already, and I can promise you, the new facility is going to be a very charming, welcome addition to the area!

AN UNNAMED COLLEGE
ADMISSIONS COUNSELOR,

*in fine spirits after an extra-long lunch
with favorite colleagues, reads the following essay
and is predisposed to like it.*

Steven T. Davinski

Personal Statement

ADMIT

*In an essay of no more than 350 words, please describe
an experience from your life when you felt like an
outsider. What did it teach you?*

Even though I am the president of our student
government, I understand better than most people how
it feels to be marginalized in society. My girlfriend
Saba is as American as me, but her parents were born
in Pakistan. Saba's family has been the victim of
unspeakable discrimination. Last fall, their home was

destroyed in a fire, which was determined to be arson.
The only explanation was that it was a hate crime. Soon
after, a valuable piece of artwork, which had been
donated specifically to raise money for Saba's family,
was stolen and then senselessly destroyed—only for
spite.

In addition, during this school year, my family
hosted a foreign exchange student from Spain. We
looked forward to Javier's arrival and welcomed him
into our home, despite his cultural differences and shy
personality. Unfortunately, the only warmth Javier
experienced during his stay was the affection our family
bestowed upon him. Javier left after one semester, when
it was clear that he did not feel like an accepted member
of the school community.

These painful experiences may help to explain my
low GPA during my senior year. In fact, I had hoped
to raise my grades as a senior, but unfortunately that
wasn't able to happen due to the impacts of prejudice
and hate in our community. However, the time
spent with my Spanish brother, as well as my close

relationship with Saba, has taught me something very important: Despite what the Constitution says, not all people in America are treated equally.

If admitted to your fine university, I plan to pursue a degree and a career that allows me to fight for the rights of all people, not just the insiders. I plan to study law, eventually working as a vocal advocate for immigrant rights. (A second option would be to work as an investment banker.)

I am normally a responsible, by-the-rules, natural leader, but the things I have seen this year compel me to raise my voice and become an activist. We must demand equality and acceptance for everyone now.

Thank you very much for considering my application.

LOUISE DENISON, INTERNATIONAL FINE ART AUTHENTICATION & APPRAISALS,

sends an email to Mr. Pierce McQueen,
United Insurance.

Dear Mr. McQueen:

Lately I have been dividing my time between Chicago and Chandigarh, India. How the mail piles up in my absence! (It is challenging to manage two completely separate lives, I am finding.) Anyway, I returned yesterday after three months abroad and found a report from you, as well as some correspondence on my desk relating to Henry Darger and what looks like an IFAAA appraisal from last fall, for a client named Monica Spoon. I do appreciate being cc'd on this claim. But the paperwork is full of errors—maybe sent to my office by mistake? It's lucky I saw this at all because I head straight back to India in a few days. I am writing to you quickly (still half-asleep with jet-lag) in the hope we may clarify this matter as soon as possible.

Around late October of last year, I received a phone call from the principal of the Highsmith School—a request for an appraisal on what might be work by Henry Darger. A day or two later, when I arrived at the school at the appointed time, a girl met me in the parking lot, a student. She greeted me by name. As we walked into the building, I said it was great they contacted me when they did, because in a couple of weeks I would be leaving on a research sabbatical. I was busy getting ready for that and not doing many new appraisals.

The girl looked at me funny. I could see she was confused. She explained that there must have been a misunderstanding: I'd been asked to come at her own request—not for an appraisal, but for a classroom research project on careers.

She said she'd seen the newspaper article about (what was then) my forthcoming trip to India to study the work of Nek Chand. She said that "outsider art" was a particular interest of hers, and she was so grateful I'd made time to come and speak with her about it.

"What about Henry Darger?" I asked—because the principal had expressly made an appointment for an appraisal. That was clear.

The girl explained that maybe the principal herself had been confused by the student's request. It was true, she said, that her interest in Darger had been born on a class trip to the Intuit museum in Chicago. That's where she got the idea to research careers in the art market, especially outsider art, etc.

I was disappointed—big understatement. I'd spent about 48 hours excited about possibly seeing something new by my beloved Henry Darger. And as I say, time was tight. So honestly it was awkward. But I figured, I'm here, and this blond girl seems sweet—so why not give her thirty minutes?

We found an empty classroom and sat down. It turned out to be a fun conversation, because this student was so prepared. She had a list of excellent, detailed questions: What are the steps one takes to authenticate valuable art? What different types of tests are conducted, and how much time is needed? What forms are used? That sort of thing. I was happy to answer all her questions. I even gave her blank copies of the forms we use to authenticate and appraise art.

Before I left, she asked me to sign the interview sheet that her teacher required, which I did. When

245

I drove away, I was impressed with the girl, but truthfully I didn't think about her again until today.

Bottom line: At no time did I see any new Darger artwork. I saw no artwork that day at all.

So now, finding this paperwork in the mail is truly confusing. Maybe someone at the Highsmith School contacted another appraiser here in Chicago? I can't imagine who. There aren't many people around who are qualified to authenticate this level of work. Even then, why would my name and signature be on this appraisal? So please, let's clarify and correct this mistake as soon as possible. I am sure we both understand the need to sort this out quickly and quietly.

Thanks.

More than a month later, on FRIDAY EVENING,
MARCH 15, the sky is clear and full of stars, and

SABA KHAN, SOPHOMORE,

retrieves the dusty notebook from under her bed in order
to add one essential epilogue.

Today after school, I found Beti waiting at my locker, hands
on her hips like I was in some kind of trouble. She reminded me
that I <u>promised</u> we would hit the courts near the condo just
as <u>soon</u> as it got <u>warm</u> outside. We've had about 5 minutes of
sun so far, but Beti tapped the time display on her phone +
pointed toward the exit, all like, "Hello?" as if the sky would
fall on our heads if we don't play soon.

Until today, I haven't been in the mood. I've been in
hibernation mode ever since winter break. But with Beti
frowning in my face like that, the idea hit me that maybe I've
been depressed or something because of all that's happened. It
was scary to imagine that things had messed with my head
more than I even thought. So I caved + told Beti we'd play
tomorrow for sure.

In the gym, Coach P was rolling a volleyball post across

the floor. When I told her I needed to grab my racket for the weekend, she called over her shoulder, "Ease into it + avoid injury!"

I let myself into the gym office, feeling suddenly strange. It was the 1st time I'd been in there since the day the paintings were stolen. The easel had been moved, closed up + now leaned against the greasy popcorn machine. I let my eyes rest on it, dreaming of what might have been, but only for a second.

My tennis racket was right where I knew it would be—the bright pink curve of the head was easy to spot in the back of the bucket.

When I pulled it out, the 1st thing I noticed was that something was fastened to the grip with a rubber band. An envelope.

I thought (weakly), a note from Steve? Yeah, right.

I pulled off the rubber band + looked at the front of the envelope. "Saba Khan ONLY" in shaky blue ink. Weird + weirder.

The envelope was sealed. Even before I tore it open, I knew: This was from Kendra. I'd actually been waiting to hear from her, anticipating a letter or an email from whatever poser's paradise she + her family have landed in. I expected some sort of confession—an honest acknowledgment of what she did. Even a simple apology along the lines of: "Yo, Saba, sorry we changed our minds + decided to keep the insurance money for ourselves. I guess we suck. See ya!" She owed me that, at least. An acknowledgment of the fact that she's a selfish, horrible person.

The envelope contained 2 folded sheets of paper: 1 of them was a note, the other a large color photograph. Computer printouts.

I looked at the photo. The quality isn't great. Cheap ink printer. The image is a tennis court, intense green, with some yellow trees in the background. Off to the right, in a loose team T-shirt + white sweatpants, me. My bright body nearly fills the frame, top to bottom. I have to say, it's an excellent shot of my backhand—perfect form, the expression on my face focused, fierce. It looks like I'm totally going to nail that sucker. Actually it's the kind of picture anyone likes to have of herself: kickass, the version of me I most want to be true.

The weirdest part was, I knew exactly which match it was. It was clear the second I looked at it. New haircut + yellow/red sweatband across my forehead = the match against Fenwick. The day of the fire.

How strange, I thought, that Kendra had this photo all the time + never showed it to me. + how insane that she would leave it for me now, after everything that's happened. As a consolation prize, this was pretty weak.

I looked at the note. I read it slowly. (Ease into it + avoid injury!) Then I read it again. It's a real work of art. It belongs here in this account.

Saba,

By tomorrow, we'll be far away from Chicago. We'll
be the "new kids" all over again. I'm not complaining.
We're used to it.

Before we go, I want you to know how sorry I am for
any grief we caused you. Seriously, it was not personal.
It could have been anyone! But you are predictable.
Your family is predictable. That was the thing, OK?

Or, that was one thing. The other thing was: People
see what they want to see. They believe what they
want to believe. Like, between you and me, there are
considerable differences between what international art
experts look like and what my mom looks like. But . . .
whatever. It's just easier for people to trust and make
stupid assumptions and expect the best out of people.
Or the worst. In any case, things went more smoothly
than we even hoped.

Only Mr. Delacroix—what a hassle! We never
expected him to act all possessive, like HE owned the
art. But he taught us something: Better keep an eye on
your valuables or you may lose them. And I feel bad
about Javier, who I genuinely liked. I did what I could
to help him, but . . . I don't know. I guess nobody gets
everything they want.

But we both did OK, didn't we? Admit: You're better off now than you were before. That condo is sick. Even your mosque got some money. That's all that should matter. Saba stock is through the roof! We both win. That's the only way to look at it.

More than anything, I'm grateful for the opportunity you gave us. Remember at the end of *Gatsby*? Nick considers the new friends he's made in New York a "rotten crowd." He calls them "careless people." Saba, I hope that after knowing us even briefly, you'll realize that we are totally the opposite. From the very beginning, nobody got hurt. We made sure of that.

Peace? Good. Now go kick some butt on the court.

No signature. No apology for keeping the insurance money. Because keeping that money was always their plan? Pathetic.

I stood in the gym office, letting this information sink in. Kendra's mother had pretended to be the art expert . . . so the paintings were fakes? Or might have been fakes? Why? Initially, the point wasn't clear to me. All I knew was, our friendship was as big a fraud as anything.

What I couldn't figure out (at 1st) was the part about me being predictable. How was that even relevant?

I folded up the note, put it back into the envelope.

I returned to the photo, my hands trembling, thinking again how random it was that Kendra had left it for me. The 2nd time I looked at it, I noticed something peculiar: It's sort of fuzzy, but dead center in the background of the image, beyond the chain-link fence + under those yellow trees, you can see Ammi + Papa sitting on the hood of the car. Salman is sitting nearby, reading a book in the grass.

So it isn't a picture of me only. It's a family portrait.

I couldn't take my eyes off that detail. How bizarre that Kendra + her stupid ladybug phone had photographed my entire family at the precise moment our lives were changing forever—before anyone could have known it.

I refolded the photo + slid it into the envelope with the note. I needed to show these things to someone.

I hurried out of the gym office, nearly forgetting my racket. I walked down the corridor + out of the building, all the time wondering: Why had she left this note for me? The girl didn't seem sorry, not really.

After all, she wasn't my friend. She only used me. That fact was so obvious now. From the beginning, she had exploited my family's tragedy for her personal gain. On some level, I knew that already. Thanks to the fundraiser, Ms. Nobody Newcomer had become Ms. Happy Highsmith in record time. Now she's rich, too. What's the difference? Same selfish person.

I nabbed the only open seat on the express bus. All the way home, my brain kept adding more questions in an unceasing loop: Why had Kendra taken this picture? Of all those matches, why that particular one? Why hadn't she shown it to me, the way she showed me the 1000 other random photos she took?

Also: Who else had seen it? On the day the photo was taken, had Kendra pressed a little button on her phone + sent it to someone? Maybe to some idiot waiting near our old apartment with turpentine, rags + matches? Someone waiting for confirmation that my entire family was safely, predictably, at the park?

Kendra's note said: "From the very beginning, nobody got hurt. We made sure of that."

Made sure _how_? . . . By calling the freaking fire department?

Like flipping a light switch in my head, I went from total ignorance to being certain. That's how sure I was. It made me feel nauseated. For several minutes, I endured this stomach-turning flashback to how I felt on the day of the fire. I leaned forward, doubled over in my seat on the bus + struggled to breathe. The commuters sitting next to me must have thought I was having a panic attack.

Could the Spoons really have started the fire? The idea brought bile to my mouth. But if it was true, it would give us 1 more answer, at least.

At supper, Ammi + Papa told me I imagined things. Even when I made them read the note, they said I should stop guessing, stop inventing. "The child feels some guilt for keeping the money, as she should," Papa said. "But she confesses to no specific crime. She admits no responsibility." When I showed him the picture again, he waved it away, saying, "You are accountable only for your deeds, for your clean heart. Not for anyone else's."

"Focus on today, not yesterday," Ammi said. "You have homework this weekend, yes? Focus on that. Let God handle the rest." She turned on the kitchen TV so that she could watch our neighbor, "Hannah from down the hall," who now works the 6:00 news. "A promotion!" Ammi brags to her friends on the old street.

Salman watches with her, eager for any stories about guns or sports or someone else's fire. That boy's dreams are such boy dreams.

Who knows what makes people act the way they do? A person could go crazy trying to figure it all out. Maybe it's better to leave those questions to the social workers of the world + to the reporters, police detectives + fire marshals. But not me.

Papa's right: The only secret motives I need to keep track of are the ones in my own heart.

For now, I've tucked the picture into the frame of my bedroom mirror. In spite of everything, I do like the way I look in it: standing at the very edge of the court, dressed in clothes my father gave me, ready to nail that ball.

Kendra's note said, "Nobody gets everything they want."

Says who?

I beat that girl from Fenwick last fall + I'll do it again this year. I'll work like hell at it, stay in shape. Starting tomorrow, Beti + I will practice all summer long at the free courts across the street. I'll tell you what's "top of mind"—winning.

Like the picture reminds me, the ball rarely comes straight to me. I have to run for it. So that's what I'll do.

ACKNOWLEDGMENTS

This outsider novel has had the support of three welcoming insiders: Elise Howard, Emily Parliman, and Jennifer Laughran. I'm grateful for the opportunity and for the generous attention they gave to this project.

The students and staff at CICS Northtown Academy in Chicago inspire me every day. For helping me to tell this story, I owe particular thanks to Imran, Maria, Nawal, Salman, Sarah, Shan, Syed, and Tooba.

The Intuit museum in Chicago, the Milwaukee Art Museum, and the American Folk Art Museum in New York are three institutions, along with many others, that preserve and lovingly exhibit the work of Henry Darger. Jessica Yu's documentary, *In the Realms of the Unreal* (Genius Entertainment, 2004), tells the fascinating story of Darger's life. The many color photographs in the book *Henry Darger's Room* (Imperial Press, 2008) provided constant inspiration during the writing of this book.

The encouragement from my family and friends is a treasure that would be worth stealing if they didn't always give it so freely. Thanks especially to Mike, my partner, who handles more than his share of the dirty work.

In August of 2008, in a hotel room in Los Angeles, my sister Kate and I stayed awake very late plotting the basic story told in this book. If more dreamers had a sister like Kate by their side, more dreams would come true. (Or more crimes, anyway.) Thank you, Kate.

THE ART OF SECRETS

Questions for Discussion

QUESTIONS FOR DISCUSSION

1. Saba Khan's Pakistani parents hold traditional beliefs—for example, fifteen-year-old Saba has to fight to play tennis, because her father objects to her wearing shorts in public. On page 123, Steve Davinski tells his friends that Saba has a whole extra set of rules to live by, like "Fit in with two cultures," "Speak two languages fluently," and "Try to look innocent." Do any members of your family or any of your friends have to fit in with more than one culture or speak more than one language? What are the benefits and challenges of being a dual-culture family?

2. On page 121, Steve says, "I've been with girls for a lot of reasons . . . And who are we kidding? Girls date me for reasons of their own, too." Describe some of the reasons Saba and Steve embark on a romantic relationship. Do they both get what they want?

3. Why do you think the author chose to write the story from multiple points of view? How would the novel have been different if only one person told the whole story—for example, Saba, or Kevin Spoon, or even one of the teachers?

4. The artist Henry Darger is known as an "outsider artist" because he created art independently, outside the known cultural establishment. *The Art of Secrets* is teeming with "outsiders"—Saba Khan with her Pakistani roots; Javier Conejera, the exchange student from Spain; Ariel Ames, the "new" English teacher who hasn't yet been accepted even after three years; Jean Delacroix, the gay art teacher who works solo; and newcomers Kendra and Kevin Spoon, who don't quite fit in with the "legacy" students at Highsmith School. Do all the outsiders in the book long to be insiders? Is anyone happy being an outsider? Are there any true insiders in the story?

5. Steve Davinski struggles to complete his college application essay because he isn't sure what to write. Ultimately, we learn, he writes about his recent experiences with Saba and Javier. How did you feel about the essay? Did it change your opinion of Steve?

6. Almost everyone in the story talks to the *Chicago Tribune* reporter at some point to tell him what "really" happened. On page 109, the principal even tries to feed the reporter the headline "We're all victims now." Based on the resulting *Tribune* articles, would you say the reporter was successfully manipulated by the principal and others?

7. When you first found out the Darger paintings were stolen, was there anyone you immediately suspected? If so, what were some clues that made you suspicious of that person? Did your mind ever change about who the thief might be? Were you surprised by the ending? Why or why not?

8. On page 173, Kevin Spoon says, "It's naïve to think that people go around helping people without some motivation, without expecting something in return, right?" Do you think it's true that people only help others if there's some selfish purpose behind it? Can you think of any examples in *The Art of Secrets* where people helped people just out of kindness?

9. Many of the characters—including Javier, Jean Delacroix, and Ariel Ames—make choices that may have surprised you. In each case, was the character justified in doing what he or she did?

10. Henry Darger's surreal paintings inspire wildly different reactions from this cast of characters. Saba finds them strange, violent, and ugly (page 98); Steve Davinski calls them "girly watercolor paintings" (page 78); and Kevin Spoon says he can relate to the images of fierce young kids who bravely take on grown-ups and defeat them (page 233). Javier says they "tell us a story of innocence and darkness" (page 133). Take a moment to do an online image search on the art of Henry Darger. What are your impressions of this outsider artist's work?

11. Which character or characters do you hold responsible for the good things and bad things that Saba has experienced this year? Do you agree with Saba's theory of what truly happened? Why or why not?

James Klise is the author of *Love Drugged,* which was an ALA Stonewall Honor Book and received glowing reviews. He lives in Chicago, where he works as a high school librarian. His short stories have appeared in many journals, including *StoryQuarterly, New Orleans Review, Ascent,* and *Southern Humanities Review. The Art of Secrets* is his second novel.